A COMPLETE COLLECTION OF GENTEEL AND INGENIOUS CONVERSATION

Jonathan Swift
(Simon Wagstaff)

With a new Introduction by the
Rt Hon. Michael Foot

THOEMMES PRESS

© Thoemmes Press 1995

Published in 1995 by
Thoemmes Press
11 Great George Street
Bristol BS1 5RR
England

ISBN 1 85506 380 8

This is a reprint of the 1755 Edition
© *Introduction* by the Rt Hon. Michael Foot 1995

Publisher's Note

These reprints are taken from original copies of each book. In many cases the condition of those originals is not perfect, the paper, often handmade, having suffered over time and the copy from such things as inconsistent printing pressures resulting in faint text, show-through from one side of a leaf to the other, the filling in of some characters, and the break up of type. The publisher has gone to great lengths to ensure the quality of these reprints but points out that certain characteristics of the original copies will, of necessity, be apparent in reprints thereof.

INTRODUCTION

Poets write the best prose. My father, who was one of the greatest readers who ever read, could make this assertion quite casually. I dare say he was quoting somebody else, as he often did, and if challenged he would resort to his infallible literary recollection. I sometimes supposed that he might have been making the claim on behalf of his best-beloved literary-cum-political hero, John Milton. He could roll *Areopagitica* round his tongue as readily as *Lycidas* or *Comus* or *Paradise Lost*. He knew how Milton himself could turn from one art to the other, with no lapse in his power, how the overriding purpose was to win the immediate battle against the enemy, and thereby to prepare for the glorious, final triumph over the forces of unrighteousness. John Milton's prose no less than his poetry were the essential weapons in this armoury, and no distinction need be drawn between the two.

So let us modify the earlier proposition: Jonathan Swift wrote the best prose. I myself would certainly be eager to sustain this judgement, and I can even imagine to myself that my much more extensively-read, knowledgeable, fair-minded father would not dissent from it. He taught me to read Swift, although he must have known better than anyone what a gulf existed between Swift's religious and political opinions and his own, and even more sharply and spectacularly between Swift's and John Milton's. He might have seen the two men as mortal enemies, and nothing else. Each prided himself on the devotion with which he would serve his chosen cause; each showed what a high passion could be brought to the political contest, whether they turned to prose or poetry for their chief instrument of the moment. No doubt my father understood that too. It was the kind of politics, the only kind of politics, in which he believed.

Twentieth-century readers have often had Jonathan Swift presented to them in this light, especially since the publication of the great Shakespeare Head edition of his works, edited by Herbert Davis in the 1950s and the 1960s. Swift had some good editors before him, but nothing to equal such a sustained feat of scholarship and sympathy. Since then, good editors, good critics, good biographers have seemed to compete with one another in enhancing still further the Swiftian renaissance. The prose writer, the poet, the politician, each seemed to help fortify the reputation of the other until the claim for his pre-eminence became widely acknowledged.

And yet we must pause at once to consider how outraged previous generations of readers would have been by any such conclusion. A century earlier Victorian England would have dismissed the Herbert Davis verdict on Swift's worth as hopelessly unbalanced: the edition itself might have been branded as too brash an offence against both the morals and the politics of that period. And Victorian England could argue that it was not at all engaged in some new censorious or puritanical exercise; it was doing no more than sustain the settled judgement of the Johnsonian England of the century before theirs, the generation that knew Swift best.

Who better indeed to judge Jonathan Swift than Dr Johnson himself? They were dealers in the same trade of words, conscious traffickers in the same business of constructing the English language and, at a most delicate period in its formation, pretenders to the same Christian faith. It is surely a matter of some moment that one practitioner in these high, kindred callings regarded the other as a clumsy, ignorant intruder, an impostor even. Swift, alas, had no chance to give his view about Johnson, but Dr Johnson constantly returned to the sore subject of Johnathan Swift. He scoffed at most of his writings, happily concurred with Dryden's verdict about his poetry – 'Cousin Swift, you will never be a poet', – dismissed *Gulliver's Travels* in terms which proved that he had never troubled to read the last two voyages, contrasted that last wretched performance so disadvantageously with *A Tale of a Tub* that he insisted the two could never have been written by the same hand, and finally portrayed the senile Swift stricken by his sins and paraded through the streets of Dublin, 'a driveller and a show'. It was these last strokes from Dr Johnson's pen which seemed indelible. He would be damned to all eternity.

And yet he survived – thanks to his literary genius, first and foremost, but thanks also to the process of rediscovery which followed quite uncharted channels. It was Swift's politics which started to win him new readers and disciples, although most people then or thereafter would dismiss his excursion into political matters as absurd, trivial or hopelessly out-of-date; he might even at times label himself a Tory, but even that could not produce a reconciliation with Dr Johnson; he was just dismissed as more mischievous than ever. Who and what was this curious specimen which insisted that politics was a business suited to many heads? He preached a kind of primitive democracy, although of course he never used the word. Everyone in Dublin could understand him, even if the Ministry in London could not. 'All government without the consent of the governed is the very definition of slavery.' That was plain enough, too plain for those in London who believed that the best of all governments had been ordained in heaven, if sanctified in London.

A growing body of readers and writers on both sides of the Irish Sea started to attribute their latest, growing political appreciation to Jonathan Swift, and none of them would seek to draw too sharp a contrast between the content and style. It was a distinguished list indeed although most of them did not start to acquire their distinction until later: Thomas Paine, author of *Common Sense* and *Rights of Man*; William Godwin, author of *Political Justice*; William Cobbett, author of *Rural Rides* and editor of *The Examiner*, named after Swift's own paper, and, most explicit and adventurous of all, William Hazlitt who led the critical attack on the Johnsonian hegemony, and developed a double interest to vindicate Swift. He adopted and adapted Swift's politics to suit his own rich brand of radicalism, honoured Swift the poet hardly less than the prose writer, and enlisted Gulliver at his side to expose all hypocrises, ancient and modern. Hazlitt's comprehensive defence and attack was delivered in a lecture at London in 1816 and then published in his *Lectures on English Poets*. After that exposition, no excuse for the persistent defamation still existed. Any traducer of Swift should have been required to answer Hazlitt. But instead the Victorian calumny was allowed to mount to its climax. The whole English establishment, Tory and

Whig, still pursued their vendetta against the Irish outcast.

One of the best modern defences, and one to set beside Hazlitt's – high praise indeed – was written by Herbert Paul in January 1900. He called his essay *The Prince of Journalists* and he fully established that claim for Swift. Yet in modern parlance that is not enough. But Herbert Paul in that same essay says enough to underline Swift's mastery in so many fields and he offers some clinching proofs of how and why he developed his own original prose style. 'Eminent statesmen', he remarked, 'had sometimes told him that politics were only common sense. It was the one thing they told him that was true, and the one they wished him not to believe.' So he developed his own common sensical politics. 'He had one of those intellects which no sophistry can delude, and which are incapable of deviating from the path of reason.' So he developed his individual style 'as a method of conveying thought it is perfect. Nothing said by Swift could ever be said again without being spoilt in the saying.... There is no veil, however thin, between the mind of the author and the mind of the public. Clearness and force could not be more harmoniously combined.' Thus Herbert Paul, in his whole essay, examined the journalistic merit of the Swiftian style, but he included also an example of a more magical gift. He quoted another sentence from another Swift, no less perfect: 'As for us, the ancients, we are content with the bee to pretend to nothing of our own beyond our wings and our voice, that is to say, our flights and our language. For the rest whatever we have got, has been by infinite labour and search, and ranging through every corner of nature. The difference is that instead of dirt and poison we have rather chosen to fill our hives with honey and wax, thus furnishing mankind with the two noblest things which are sweetness and light.' Those sentences may not be accepted as typically Swiftian, yet he could always guide his readers with his rhythms. His political tracts were infused with the same humanity.

Was not the prince of journalists also a great artist? It would be hard to deny him the distinction, even though he never claimed it for himself. What he did, for sure, despite the Dryden discouragement, was to make himself into a great poet, recognized as such by the foremost critics such as Hazlitt, or his foremost fellow-poets, such as Byron, or some of the foremost statesmen of that age, such as Charles James Fox, who had received a proper education at their fathers' knees in literary no less than political questions. None of these who knew and loved him best would draw too sharp a distinction between his prose and his poetry and his polemics. And he himself seemed to share this understanding of what literature could be. When the authorities at Oxford University, conscious maybe of their own failure to recognize the talents of a younger Jonathan Swift, asked him for a gift he sent them not one of his learned treatises on the Christian religion or the English language but the most potently revolutionary of his Irish tracts:

> FRAUD DETECTED OR THE HIBERNIAN PATRIOT, Containing, All the Drapier's Letters to the People of Ireland, on Words, Coinage etc. ...Also, a new Poem to the Drapier And Songs sung at the Drapier's Club in Thick Street, Dublin, never before printed. With a PREFACE explaining the Usefulness of the Whole – Humbly presented to the Bodleyan Library in Oxford by M. B. Drapier.

Thus Swift himself would merge together his gifts, and the best of his editors would not seek to disentangle them. Another of the good critics in this century saw the relationship in a similar revelation. He was writing about Byron, but the kinship between them – and the third in the great triumvirate – came at once to his mind:

> His political activity began with his departure from Venice for Ravenna; and he was prepared to go to all lengths had not the Italians recoiled. The expedition to Greece was not the outcome of a sudden impulse to escape from idleness and ennui. It was a second chapter in the history of his endeavour to serve the cause of emancipation with his sword as well as his pen. Milton and Swift are the only other Englishmen of Letters whose writings have been not only literary works but deeds. The former exercised but little influence on the actual course of events, but a careful study of his last poems in relation to the political pamphlets and *De Doctrina* will show that they were more to their author than works of art alone. They were great political acts; declarations by the poet intended to be trumpet-calls to action, a vindication of freedom conceived as obedience to reason and reason only, addressed to the English people and the Christian world, and if they failed to find such hearing as he desired, yet before *Paradise Lost* had been published Milton's name had a European reputation, 'and the only inducement of several foreigners that came over into England was chiefly to see Oliver Protector and Mr John Milton'. Swift was a pamphleteer, but his pamphlets ended a European war and shook the government of Ireland, and it was not the satire alone which did so but the personality,

the fearless pride and strength of the man who launched them. And Byron's voice rang through Europe....'

Professor Grierson

Such a specious view of Swift's political vision – a hint of his influence in the Europe which he never visited – might seem a strange introduction to one of his pieces of writing most consciously directed to the characters in his own small world which he would dissect with a mordant fascination. Yet his own introduction is the best reply. Read the whole of it and then re-read it, and then, maybe learn the futility, as mentioned by Herbert Paul, of attempting to alter the sentences.

The comparison between Swift and either Milton or Byron may at first seem too startling to be valid. Apart from other distinctions, they each had a revolutionary faith to sustain which we can acclaim today. Milton believed that the forces of evil would be finally defeated in some 'endless, restless change' of near-Marxist spaciousness: 'if this fail, the pillared firmament is rottenness / And earth's base built on stubble.' Byron, too, whatever the setbacks, would always assert the final victory: 'Freedom's battle once begun, Bequeathed from bleeding sire to son / Though baffled oft is ever won.'

Swift had no such doctrine to which he could hold fast, amid all the storms. Certainly he made no avowal of any religious faith to match Milton's and Byron's assurance that the revolutionary defeats of their epochs would not last for ever. Each of them chose the most appropriate form to assert with sufficient force the opposite conclusion. To suit the needs of their own times, they both wrote epics. Swift could not or would not do the same; he had no such world vision. But in a sense this disqualification makes his achievement all the greater. He was not prepared to abandon his faith in humankind: mankind and womankind. His poetry and his prose were directed to this end. Taken together they produced the fearless pride and strength of the man who served liberty no less than the other two.

His *Gulliver* takes its place beside Byron's *Don Juan* or Milton's *Paradise Lost* and his *Polite Conversations* can still offer a special introduction to the whole Swiftian world.

Michael Foot
1995

A COMPLETE

COLLECTION

Of Genteel and Ingenious

CONVERSATION,

According to the moſt

Polite Mode and Method

NOW USED

At COURT, and in the Best Companies
OF *ENGLAND*.

IN THREE DIALOGUES.

By *SIMON WAGSTAFF*, Eſq;

AN INTRODUCTION[*].

AS my life hath been chiefly spent in consulting the honour and welfare of my country for more than forty years past, not without answerable success, if the world and my friends have not flattered me; so there is no point wherein I have so much laboured, as that of improving and polishing all parts of conversation between persons of quality, whether they meet by accident or invitation, at meals, tea, or visits, mornings, noons, or evenings.

I have passed perhaps more time than any other man of my age and country in

---

[*] This treatise appears to have been written with the same view, as the *tritical essay on the faculties of the mind*, but upon a more general plan: the ridicule, which is there confined to literary composition, is here extended to conversation, but its object is the same in both; the repetition of quaint phrases picked up by rote either from the living or the dead, and applied upon every occasion to conceal ignorance or stupidity, or to prevent the labour of thoughts to produce native sentiment, and combine such words as will precisely express it.

visits and assemblies, where the polite persons of both sexes distinguish themselves; and could not without much grief observe how frequently both gentlemen and ladies are at a loss for questions, answers, replies and rejoinders. However, my concern was much abated, when I found that these defects were not occasioned by any want of materials, but because those materials were not in every hand: for instance, one lady can give an answer better than ask a question: one gentleman is happy at a reply; another excels in a rejoinder: one can revive a languishing conversation by a sudden surprizing sentence; another is more dextrous in seconding; a third can fill the gap with laughing, or commending what has been said: thus fresh hints may be started, and the ball of the discourse kept up.

But alas! this is too seldom the case, even in the most select companies. How often do we see at court, at publick visiting-days, at great men's levees, and other places of general meeting, that the conversation falls and drops to nothing, like a fire without supply of fuel. This is what
we

INTRODUCTION.

we all ought to lament; and againſt this dangerous evil I take upon me to affirm, that I have in the following papers provided an infallible remedy.

It was in the year 1695, and the ſixth of his late majeſty King WILLIAM the Third of ever glorious and immortal memory, who reſcued three kingdoms from popery and ſlavery, when, being about the age of ſix-and-thirty, my judgment mature, of good reputation in the world, and well acquainted with the beſt families in town, I determined to ſpend five mornings, to dine four times, paſs three afternoons, and ſix evenings every week, in the houſes of the moſt polite families, of which I would confine myſelf to fifty; only changing as the maſters or ladies died, or left the town, or grew out of vogue, or ſunk in their fortunes, or (which to me was of the higheſt moment) became diſaffected to the government; which practice I have followed ever ſince to this very day; except when I happened to be ſick, or in the ſpleen upon cloudy weather; and except when I entertained four of each fex at my own lodgings once in a month, by way of retaliation.

I always kept a large table-book in my pocket; and as foon as I left the company, I immediately entered the choiceft expreffions that paffed during the vifit; which, returning home, I tranfcribed in a fair hand, but fomewhat enlarged; and had made the greateft part of my collection in twelve years, but not digefted into any method; for this I found was a work of infinite labour, and what required the niceft judgment, and confequently could not be brought to any degree of perfection in lefs than fixteen years more.

Herein I refolved to exceed the advice of *Horace*, a *Roman* poet, which I have read in Mr. *Creech*'s admirable tranflation; that an author fhould keep his works nine years in his clofet, before he ventured to publifh them: and finding that I ftill received fome additional flowers of wit and language, although in a very fmall number, I determined to defer the publication, to purfue my defign, and exhauft if poffible the whole fubject, that I might

INTRODUCTION.

might present a complete system to the world; for, I am convinced by long experience, that the critics will be as severe as their old envy against me can make them: I foresee they will object, that I have inserted many answers and replies which are neither witty, humorous, polite, nor authentic; and have omitted others that would have been highly useful, as well as entertaining. But let them come to particulars, and I will boldly engage to confute their malice.

For these last six or seven years I have not been able to add above nine valuable sentences to enrich my collection: from whence I conclude, that what remains will amount only to a trifle. However, if, after the publication of this work, any lady or gentleman, when they have read it, shall find the least thing of importance omitted, I desire they will please to supply my defects by communicating to me their discoveries; and their letters may be directed to Simon Wagstaff, Esq; at his lodgings next door to the *Gloucester-head* in St. *James's-street*, (paying the postage.) In return of which favour, I shall

shall make honourable mention of their names in a short preface to the second edition.

In the mean time, I cannot but with some pride, and much pleasure, congratulate with my dear country, which hath outdone all the nations of *Europe*, in advancing the whole art of conversation to the greatest heighth it is capable of reaching; and therefore, being intirely convinced that the collection I now offer to the publick is full and complete, I may at the same time boldly affirm, that the whole genius, humour, politeness, and eloquence of *England* are summed up in it : nor is the treasure small, wherein are to be found at least a thousand shining questions, answers, repartees, replies and rejoinders, fitted to adorn every kind of discourse that an assembly of *English* ladies and gentlemen, met together for their mutual entertainment, can possibly want : especially when the several flowers shall be set off and improved by the speakers, with every circumstance of preface and circumlocution, in proper terms; and attended with praise, laughter or admiration.

There

INTRODUCTION.

There is a natural, involuntary diftortion of the mufcles, which is the anatomical caufe of laughter; but there is another caufe of laughter which decency requires, and is the undoubted mark of a good tafte, as well as of a polite obliging behaviour; neither is this to be acquired without much obfervation, long practice, and a found judgment; I did therefore once intend, for the eafe of the learner, to fet down in all parts of the following dialogues certain marks, afterifks, or *nota-bene's* (in *Englifh, Markwell's*) after moft queftions, and every reply or anfwer; directing exactly the moment when one, two, or all the company are to laugh: but having duly confidered, that this expedient would too much enlarge the bulk of the volume, and confequently the price; and likewife that fomething ought to be left for ingenious readers to find out, I have determined to leave that whole affair, although of great importance, to their own difcretion.

The reader muft learn by all means to diftinguifh between proverbs and thofe polite fpeeches which beautify converfation:

tion: for, as to the former, I utterly reject them out of all ingenious difcourfe. I acknowledge indeed, that there may poffibly be found in this treatife a few fayings, among fo great a number of fmart turns of wit and humour as I have produced, which have a proverbial air: however, I hope it will be confidered, that even thefe were not originally proverbs, but the genuine productions of fuperior wits to embellifh and fupport converfation; from whence, with great impropriety as well as plagiarifm (if you will forgive a hard word) they have moft injurioufly been transferred into proverbial maxims; and therefore in juftice ought to be refumed out of vulgar hands to adorn the drawing-rooms of princes both male and female, the levees of great minifters, as well as the toilet and tea-table of the ladies.

I can faithfully affure the reader, that there is not one fingle witty phrafe in this whole collection, which hath not received the ftamp and approbation of at leaft one hundred years, and how much longer it is hard to determine; he may therefore be

INTRODUCTION. 107

be secure to find them all genuine, sterling, and authentic.

But before this elaborate treatise can become of universal use and ornament to my native country, two points, that will require time and much application, are absolutely necessary.

For, first, whatever person would aspire to be completely witty, smart, humorous, and polite, must by hard labour be able to retain in his memory every single sentence contained in this work, so as never to be once at a loss in applying the right answers, questions, repartees, and the like, immediately, and without study or hesitation.

And, secondly, after a lady or gentleman hath so well overcome this difficulty, as never to be at a loss upon any emergency, the true management of every feature, and almost of every limb, is equally necessary; without which an infinite number of absurdities will inevitably ensue. For instance, there is hardly a polite sentence in the following dialogues which doth not absolutely require some peculiar graceful motion in the eyes, or nose, or mouth, or forehead, or chin, or suitable

tofs

toss of the head, with certain offices assigned to each hand; and in ladies, the whole exercise of the fan, fitted to the energy of every word they deliver; by no means omitting the various turns and cadence of the voice, the twistings, and movements, and different postures of the body, the several kinds and gradations of laughter, which the ladies must daily practise by the looking-glass, and consult upon them with their waiting-maids.

My readers will soon observe what a great compass of real and useful knowledge this science includes; wherein, although nature, assisted by a genius, may be very instrumental, yet a strong memory and constant application, together with example and precept, will be highly necessary. For these reasons I have often wished, that certain male and female instructors, perfectly versed in this science, would set up schools for the instruction of young ladies and gentlemen therein.

I remember about thirty years ago, there was a *Bohemian* woman, of that species commonly known by the name of *gypsies*, who came over hither from *France*,

and

INTRODUCTION.

and generally attended Isaac the dancing mafter, when he was teaching his art to miffes of quality; and while the young ladies were thus employed, the *Bohemian*, ftanding at fome diftance, but full in their fight, acted before them all proper airs, and heavings of the head, and motions of the hands, and twiftings of the body; whereof you may ftill obferve the good effects in feveral of our elder ladies.

After the fame manner, it were much to be defired, that fome expert gentlewomen gone to decay would fet up publick fchools, wherein young girls of quality, or great fortunes, might firft be taught to repeat this following fyftem of converfation, which I have been at fo much pains to compile; and then to adapt every feature of their countenances, every turn of their hands, every fcrewing of their bodies, every exercife of their fans, to the humour of the fentences they hear or deliver in converfation. But above all to inftruct them in every fpecies and degree of laughing in the proper feafons at their own wit, or that of the company. And, if the fons of the nobility and gentry, inftead of being fent to common schools, or put into the hands of tutors at home, to learn nothing but words, were consigned to able instructors in the same art, I cannot find what use there could be of books, except in the hands of those who are to make learning their trade, which is below the dignity of persons born to titles or estates.

It would be another infinite advantage, that by cultivating this science we should wholly avoid the vexations and impertinence of pedants, who affect to talk in a language not to be understood; and whenever a polite person offers accidentally to use any of their jargon-terms, have the presumption to laugh at us for pronouncing those words in a genteeler manner. Whereas, I do here affirm, that, whenever any fine gentleman or lady condescends to let a hard word pass out of their mouths, every syllable is smoothed and polished in the passage; and it is a true mark of politeness, both in writing and reading, to vary the orthography as well as the sound; because we are infinitely better judges of what will please a distinguishing ear than those who call themselves *scholars*, can possibly

INTRODUCTION.

possibly be; who, consequently, ought to correct their books, and manner of pronouncing, by the authority of our example, from whose lips they proceed with infinitely more beauty and significancy.

But, in the mean time, until so great, so useful, and so necessary a design can be put in execution, (which, considering the good disposition of our country at present, I shall not despair of living to see) let me recommend the following treatise to be carried about as a pocket-companion, by all gentlemen and ladies, when they are going to visit, or dine, or drink tea; or where they happen to pass the evening without cards, (as I have sometimes known it to be the case upon disappointments or accidents unforeseen) desiring they would read their several parts in their chairs or coaches, to prepare themselves for every kind of conversation that can possibly happen.

Although I have, in justice to my country, allowed the genius of our people to excel that of any other nation upon earth, and have confirmed this truth by an argument not to be controuled, I mean,

mean, by producing so great a number of witty sentences in the ensuing dialogues, all of undoubted authority, as well as of our own production, yet I must confess at the same time, that we are wholly indebted for them to our ancestors; at least, for as long as my memory reacheth, I do not recollect one new phrase of importance to have been added; which defect in us moderns I take to have been occasioned by the introduction of cant-words in the reign of King CHARLES the Second. And those have so often varied, that hardly one of them, of above a year's standing, is now intelligible; nor any where to be found, excepting a small number strewed here and there in the comedies and other fantastick writings of that age.

The honourable colonel JAMES GRAHAM, my old friend and companion, did likewise, towards the end of the same reign, invent a set of words and phrases, which continued almost to the time of his death. But, as these terms of art were adapted only to courts and politicians, and extended little farther than among his

parti-

particular acquaintance (of whom I had the honour to be one) they are now almoſt forgotten.

Nor did the late D. of *R-----* and E. of *E---* ſucceed much better, although they proceeded no farther than ſingle words; whereof, except *bite, bamboozle,* and one or two more, the whole vocabulary is antiquated.

The ſame fate hath already attended thoſe other town-wits, who furniſh us with a great variety of new terms, which are annually changed, and thoſe of the laſt ſeaſon ſunk in oblivion. Of theſe I was once favoured with a complete liſt by the right honourable the lord and lady *H----,* with which I made a conſiderable figure one ſummer in the country; but returning up to town in winter, and venturing to produce them again, I was partly hooted, and partly not underſtood.

The only invention of late years, which hath any way contributed towards politeneſs in diſcourſe, is that of abbreviating or reducing words of many ſyllables into one, by lopping off the reſt. This refinement having begun about the time of the *Revolution*, I had some share in the honour of promoting it, and I observe to my great satisfaction, that it makes daily advancements, and I hope in time will raise our language to the utmost perfection; although I must confess, to avoid obscurity I have been very sparing of this ornament in the following dialogues.

But, as for phrases invented to cultivate conversation, I defy all the clubs of coffee-houses in this town to invent a new one equal in wit, humour, smartness, or politeness, to the very worst of my set; which clearly shews, either that we are much degenerated, or that the whole stock of materials hath been already employed. I would willingly hope, as I do confidently believe, the latter; because, having myself for several months racked my invention to enrich this treasure (if possible) with some additions of my own (which however should have been printed in a different character, that I might not be charged with imposing upon the publick) and having shewn them to some judicious friends, they dealt very sincerely with me, all unanimously agreeing that mine were
infi-

INTRODUCTION.

infinitely below the true old helps to discourse drawn up in my present collection, and confirmed their opinion with reasons, by which I was perfectly convinced, as well as ashamed of my great presumption.

But I lately met a much stronger argument to confirm me in the same sentiments: for, as the great bishop BURNET of *Salisbury* informs us in the preface to his admirable *History of his own Times*, that he intended to employ himself in polishing it every day of his life, (and indeed in its kind it is almost equally polished with this work of mine) so it hath been my constant business for some years past to examine with the utmost strictness, whether I could possibly find the smallest lapse in style or propriety through my whole collection, that in emulation with the bishop I might send it abroad as the most finished piece of the age.

It happened one day as I was dining in good company of both sexes, and watching according to my custom for new materials wherewith to fill my pocket-book, I succeeded well enough till after dinner, when the ladies retired to their tea, and left us over a bottle of wine. But I found we were not able to furnish any more materials that were worth the pains of transcribing: for the discourse of the company was all degenerated into smart sayings of their own invention, and not of the true old standard; so that in absolute despair I withdrew, and went to attend the ladies at their tea: from whence I did then conclude, and still continue to believe, either that wine doth not inspire politeness, or that our sex is not able to support it without the company of women, who never fail to lead us into the right way, and there to keep us.

It much encreaseth the value of these apothegms, that unto them we owe the continuance of our language for at least an hundred years; neither is this to be wondred at, because indeed, besides the smartness of the wit, and fineness of the raillery, such is the propriety and energy of expression in them all, that they never can be changed, but to disadvantage, except in the circumstance of using abbreviations: which however I do not despair

INTRODUCTION.

spair in due time to see introduced, having already met them at some of the choice companies in town.

Although this work be calculated for all persons of quality and fortune of both sexes; yet the reader may perceive, that my particular view was to the *officers* of the *army*, the *gentlemen* of the *inns* of *court*, and of *both* the *universities*; to all *courtiers*, male and female, but principally to the *maids* of *honour*, of whom I have been personally acquainted with two and twenty sets, all excelling in this noble endowment; till for some years past, I know not how, they came to degenerate into selling of *bargains* and *freethinking*; not that I am against either of these entertainments at proper seasons in compliance with company, who may want a taste for more exalted discourse, whose memories may be short, who are too young to be perfect in their lessons, or (although it be hard to conceive) who have no inclination to read and learn my instructions. And besides, there is a strong temptation for court ladies to fall into the two amusements above-mentioned, that they

they may avoid the cenfure of affecting fingularity againſt the general current and faſhion of all about them: but however no man will pretend to affirm that either *bargains* or *blaſphemy*, which are the principal ornaments of *free-thinking*, are ſo good a fund of polite diſcourſe, as what is to be met with in my collection. For as to *bargains*, few of them ſeem to be excellent in their kind, and have not much variety, becauſe they all terminate in one ſingle point; and to multiply them would require more invention than people have to ſpare. And as to *blaſphemy* or *free-thinking*, I have known ſome ſcrupulous perſons of both ſexes, who by a prejudiced education are afraid of ſprights. I muſt however except the *maids* of *honour*, who have been fully convinced by a famous court-chaplain, that there is no ſuch place as hell.

I cannot indeed controvert the lawfulneſs of *free-thinking*, becauſe it hath been univerſally allowed, that thought is free. But however, although it may afford a large field of matter, yet in my poor opinion it ſeems to contain very little of

INTRODUCTION.

of wit or humour; becaufe it hath not been ancient enough among us to furnifh eftablifhed authentick expreffions, I mean fuch as muft receive a fanction from the polite world, before their authority can be allowed; neither was the art of *blaf-phemy* or *free-thinking* invented by the court, or by perfons of great quality, who properly fpeaking were patrons, rather than inventors of it; but firft brought in by the fanatick faction towards the end of their power, and after the reftoration carried to *Whitehall* by the converted *rumpers*, with very good reafon; becaufe they knew, that King CHARLES the Second from a wrong education, occafioned by the troubles of his father, had time enough to obferve, that fanatick enthufiafm directly led to atheifm, which agreed with the diffolute inclinations of his youth; and perhaps thefe principles were farther cultivated in him by the *French* Hugonots, who have been often charged with fpreading them among us: however, I cannot fee where the neceffity lies of introducing new and foreign topicks for converfation, while we have so plentiful a stock of our own growth.

I have likewise for some reasons of equal weight been very sparing in *double entendres:* because they often put ladies upon affected constraints, and affected ignorance. In short, they break, or very much entangle the thread of discourse; neither am I master of any rules to settle the disconcerted countenances of the females in such a juncture; I can therefore, only allow *inuendoes* of this kind to be delivered in whispers, and only to young ladies under twenty, who being in honour obliged to blush, it may produce a new subject for discourse.

Perhaps the criticks may accuse me of a defect in my following system of *Polite Conversation*; that there is one great ornament of discourse, whereof I have not produced a single example; which indeed I purposely omitted for some reasons that I shall immediately offer; and if those reasons will not satisfy the male part of my gentle readers, the defect may be supplied in some manner by an *appendix* to the *second edition*; which *appendix*

INTRODUCTION.

dix shall be printed by itself, and sold for *six-pence*, stitched, and with a marble cover, that my readers may have no occasion to complain of being defrauded.

The defect I mean is, my not having inserted into the body of my book, all the *oaths* now most in fashion for embellishing discourse; especially since it could give no offence to the *clergy*, who are seldom or never admitted to these polite assemblies. And it must be allowed, that oaths well chosen are not only very useful expletives to matter, but great ornaments of style.

What I shall here offer in my own defence upon this important article will, I hope, be some extenuation of my fault.

First, I reasoned with myself, that a just collection of oaths, repeated as often as the fashion requires, must have enlarged this volume at least to double the bulk; whereby it would not only double the charge, but likewise make the volume less commodious for pocket-carriage.

Secondly, I have been assured by some judicious friends, that themselves have known certain ladies to take offence
(whe-

(whether ſeriouſly or no) at too great a profuſion of curſing and ſwearing, even when that kind of ornament was not improperly introduced; which, I confeſs, did ſtartle me not a little, having never obſerved the like in the compaſs of my own ſeveral acquaintance, at leaſt for twenty years paſt. However, I was forced to ſubmit to wiſer judgments than my own.

Thirdly, as this moſt uſeful treatiſe is calculated for all future times, I conſidered in this maturity of my age, how great a variety of oaths I have heard ſince I began to ſtudy the world, and to know men and manners. And here I found it to be true, what I have read in an ancient poet.

For now a days men change their oaths,
As often as they change their cloaths.

In ſhort, oaths are the children of faſhion; they are in ſome ſenſe almoſt annuals, like what I obſerved before of cant-words; and I myſelf can remember about forty different ſets. The old ſtock-oaths, I am confident, do not amount to above forty-five,

INTRODUCTION. 123

five, or fifty at moſt; but the way of mingling and compounding them is almoſt as various as that of the alphabet.

Sir JOHN PERROT was the firſt man of quality, whom I find upon record to have ſworn by *God's wounds*. He lived in the reign of Q. ELIZABETH, and was ſuppoſed to have been a natural ſon of HENRY the Eighth, who might alſo probably have been his inſtructor. This oath indeed ſtill continues, and is a ſtock-oath to this day; ſo do ſeveral others that have kept their natural ſimplicity: but infinitely the greater number hath been ſo frequently changed and diſlocated, that if the inventors were now alive, they could hardly underſtand them.

Upon theſe conſiderations I began to apprehend, that if I ſhould inſert all the oaths that are now current, my book would be out of vogue with the firſt change of faſhion, and grow as uſeleſs as an old dictionary: whereas, the caſe is quite otherwiſe with my collection of polite diſcourſe; which, as I before obſerved, hath deſcended by tradition for at leaſt an hundred years without any change

INTRODUCTION.

change in the phraseology. I therefore determined with myself to leave out the whole system of swearing; because both the male and female oaths are all perfectly well known and distinguished; new ones are easily learnt, and with a moderate share of discretion may be properly applied on every fit occasion. However, I must here upon this article of swearing most earnestly recommend to my male readers, that they would please a little to study variety. For it is the opinion of our most refined swearers, that the same oath or curse cannot, consistently with true politeness, be repeated above nine times in the same company by the same person and at one sitting.

I am far from desiring, or expecting, that all the polite and ingenious speeches contained in this work should in the general conversation between ladies and gentlemen come in so quick and so close, as I have here delivered them. By no means: on the contrary, they ought to be husbanded better, and spread much thinner. Nor do I make the least question, but that by a discreet and thrifty manage-

INTRODUCTION.

management they may ferve for the entertainment of a whole year to any perfon, who does not make too long or too frequent vifits in the fame family. The flowers of wit, fancy, wifdom, humour, and politenefs, fcattered in this volume amount to one thoufand feventy and four, Allowing then to every gentleman and lady thirty vifiting families, (not infifting upon fractions) there will want but little of an hundred polite queftions, anfwers, replies, rejoinders, repartees, and remarks, to be daily delivered frefh in every company for twelve folar months; and even this is a higher pitch of delicacy than the world infifts on, or hath reafon to expect. But I am altogether for exalting this fcience to its utmoft perfection.

It may be objected, that the publication of my book may in a long courfe of time proftitute this noble art to mean and vulgar people; but I anfwer, that it is not fo eafy an acquirement as a few ignorant pretenders may imagine. A footman can fwear, but he cannot fwear like a lord. He can fwear as often; but, can he fwear with equal delicacy, propriety, and judgment?

ment? No certainly, unless he be a lad of superior parts, of good memory, a diligent observer, one who hath a skilful ear, some knowledge in musick, and an exact taste; which hardly fall to the share of one in a thousand among that fraternity, in as high favour as they now stand with their ladies. Neither hath one footman in six so fine a genius as to relish and apply those exalted sentences comprised in this volume, which I offer to the world. It is true, I cannot see that the same ill consequences would follow from the waiting-woman, who, if she had been bred to read romances, may have some small subaltern or second-hand politeness; and if she constantly attends the tea, and be a good listner, may in some years make a tolerable figure, which will serve perhaps to draw in the young chaplain or the old steward. But alas! after all, how can she acquire those hundred graces and motions, and airs, the whole military management of the fan, the contortions of every muscular motion in the face, the risings and fallings, the quickness and slowness of the voice, with the

INTRODUCTION.

the several turns and cadences; the proper junctures of smiling and frowning, how often and how loud to laugh, when to jibe and when to flout, with all the other branches of doctrine and discipline above recited?

I am therefore not under the least apprehension, that this art will ever be in danger of falling into common hands, which requires so much time, study, practice, and genius, before it arrives to perfection; and therefore I must repeat my proposal for erecting publick schools, provided with the best and ablest masters and mistresses at the charge of the nation.

I have drawn this work into the form of a dialogue after the pattern of other famous writers in history, law, politicks, and most other arts and sciences, and I hope it will have the same success: for, who can contest it to be of greater consequence to the happiness of these kingdoms, than all human knowledge put together? Dialogue is held the best method of inculcating any part of knowledge; and I am confident, that publick schools

will

will soon be founded for teaching wit and politeneſs after my ſcheme to young people of quality and fortune. I have determined next ſeſſions to deliver a petition to the *Houſe of Lords* for an act of parliament to eſtabliſh my book as the ſtandard *Grammar* in all the principal cities of the kingdom, where this art is to be taught by able maſters, who are to be approved and recommended by me; which is no more than LILLY obtained only for teaching words in a language wholly uſeleſs. Neither ſhall I be ſo far wanting to myſelf as not to deſire a patent, granted of courſe to all uſeful projectors; I mean, that I may have the ſole profit of giving a licence to every ſchool to read my *Grammar* for fourteen years.

The reader cannot but obſerve what pains I have been at in poliſhing the ſtyle of my book to the greateſt exactneſs: nor have I been leſs diligent in refining the orthography by ſpelling the words in the very ſame manner as they are pronounced by the chief patterns of politeneſs at court, at levees, at aſſemblies, at playhouſes, at the prime viſiting places, by young

INTRODUCTION. 129

young templers, and by gentlemen-commoners of both univerfities, who have lived at leaft a twelvemonth in town, and kept the beft company. Of thefe fpellings the publick will meet with many examples in the following book. For inftance, *can't, han't, fhan't, did'nt, coud'nt, woudn't, isn't, e'nt,* with many more; befides feveral words which fcholars pretend are derived from *Greek* and *Latin*, but now pared into a polite found by ladies, officers of the army, courtiers and templers, fuch as *jommetry* for *geometry, verdi* for *verdict, lard* for *lord, learnen* for *learning*; together with fome abbreviations exquifitely refined; as, *pozz* for *pofitive*; *mobb* for *mobile*; *phizz* for *phyfiognomy*; *rep* for *reputation*; *plenipo* for *plenipotentiary*; *incog* for *incognito*; *hypps*, or *hippo*, for *hypocondriacs*; *bam* for *bamboozle*; and *bamboozle* for *God knows what*; whereby much time is faved, and the high road to converfation cut fhort by many a mile.

I have, as it will be apparent, laboured very much, and, I hope, with felicity enough,

nough, to make every character in the dialogue agreeable with itself to a degree, that, whenever any judicious person shall read my book aloud for the entertainment and instruction of a select company, he need not so much as name the particular speakers; because all the persons throughout the several subjects of conversation strictly observe a different manner peculiar to their characters, which are of different kinds: but this I leave entirely to the prudent and impartial reader's discernment.

Perhaps the very manner of introducing the several points of wit and humour may not be less entertaining and instructing than the matter itself. In the latter I can pretend to little merit; because it entirely depends upon memory and the happiness of having kept polite company: but the art of contriving that those speeches should be introduced naturally, as the most proper sentiments to be delivered upon so great a variety of subjects, I take to be a talent somewhat uncommon, and a labour that few people could hope to succeed in, unless they had a genius particularly turned that way, added to a sincere disinterested love of the publick.

Although every curious question, smart answer, and witty reply be little known to many people, yet there is not one single sentence in the whole collection, for which I cannot bring most authentick vouchers, whenever I shall be called: and even for some expressions, which to a few nice ears may perhaps appear somewhat gross, I can produce the stamp of authority from courts, chocolate-houses, theatres, assemblies, drawing-rooms, levees, cardmeetings, balls and masquerades, from persons of both sexes, and of the highest titles next to royal. However, to say the truth, I have been very sparing in my quotations of such sentiments that seem to be over free; because, when I began my collection, such kind of converse was almost in its infancy, till it was taken into the protection of my honoured patronesses at court, by whose countenance and sanction it hath become a choice flower in the nosegay of wit and politeness.

Some will perhaps object, that when I bring my company to dinner, I mention too great a variety of dishes, not always consistent with the art of cookery, or proper for the season of the year, and part of the first course mingled with the second, besides a failure in politeness by introducing a black pudden to a lord's table, and at a great entertainment: but, if I had omitted the black pudden, I desire to know what would have become of that exquisite reason given by Miss NOTABLE for not eating it; the world perhaps might have lost it for ever, and I should have been justly answerable for having left it out of my collection. I therefore cannot but hope, that such hypercritical readers will please to consider, my business was to make so full and complete a body of refined sayings as compact as I could, only taking care to produce them in the most natural and probable manner, in order to allure my readers into the very substance and marrow of this most admirable and necessary art.

I am

INTRODUCTION.

I am heartily forry, and was much difappointed to find, that fo univerfal and polite an entertainment as CARDS hath hitherto contributed very little to the enlargement of my work. I have fate by many hundred times with the utmoft vigilance, and my table-book ready, without being able in eight hours to gather matter for one fingle phrafe in my book. But this, I think, may be eafily accounted for by the turbulence and juftling of paffions upon the various and furprizing turns, incidents, revolutions, and events of good and evil fortune, that arrive in the courfe of a long evening at play; the mind being wholly taken up, and the confequences of non-attention fo fatal.

Play is fupported upon the two great pillars of deliberation and action. The terms of art are few, prefcribed by law and cuftom; no time allowed for digreffions or trials of wit. *Quadrille* in particular bears fome refemblance to a ftate of nature, which we are told is a ftate of war, wherein every woman is againft every woman; the unions fhort, inconftant, stant, and soon broke; the league made this minute without knowing the ally, and diffolved in the next. Thus, at the game of *quadrille*, female brains are always employed in ftratagem, or their hands in action. Neither can I find, that our art hath gained much by the happy revival of *mafquerading* among us; the whole dialogue in thofe meetings being fummed up in one (fprightly, I confefs, but) fingle queftion, and as fprightly an anfwer. *Do you know me? yes, I do.* And, *Do you know me? Yes, I do.* For this reafon I did not think it proper to give my readers the trouble of introducing a mafquerade, merely for the fake of a fingle queftion, and a fingle anfwer. Efpecially when to perform this in a proper manner I muft have brought in a hundred perfons together, of both fexes, dreffed in fantaftick habits for one minute, and difmifs them the next.

Neither is it reafonable to conceive, that our fcience can be much improved by mafquerades, where the wit of both fexes is altogether taken up in contriving
fin-

singular and humoursome disguises; and their thoughts entirely employed in bringing intrigues and assignations of gallantry to an happy conclusion.

The judicious reader will readily discover, that I make Miss NOTABLE my heroine, and Mr. THOMAS NEVEROUT my hero. I have laboured both their characters with my utmost ability. It is into their mouths that I have put the liveliest questions, answers, repartees, and rejoinders; because my design was to propose them both as patterns for all young batchelors and single ladies to copy after. By which I hope very soon to see polite conversation flourish between both sexes in a more consummate degree of perfection, than these kingdoms have yet ever known.

I have drawn some lines of Sir JOHN LINGER's character, the *Derbyshire* knight, on purpose to place it in counterview or contrast with that of the other company; wherein I can assure the reader, that I intended not the least reflection upon *Derbyshire*, the place of my nativity. But my intention was only to shew

shew the misfortune of those persons, who have the disadvantage to be bred out of the circle of politeness, whereof I take the present limits to extend no further than *London*, and ten miles round; although others are pleased to confine it within the bills of mortality. If you compare the discourses of my gentlemen and ladies with those of Sir JOHN, you will hardly conceive him to have been bred in the same climate, or under the same laws, language, religion, or government: and accordingly I have introduced him speaking in his own rude dialect, for no other reason than to teach my scholars how to avoid it.

The curious reader will observe, that when conversation appears in danger to flag, which in some places I have artfully contrived, I took care to invent some sudden question, or turn of wit to revive it; such as these that follow: *What? I think here's a silent meeting! Come, madam, a penny for your thought*; with several other of the like sort. I have rejected all provincial or country turns of wit and fancy, because I am acquainted with

very

INTRODUCTION. 137

very few; but indeed chiefly, becaufe I found them fo much inferior to thofe at court, efpecially among the gentlemen ufhers, the ladies of the bed-chamber, and the maids of honour; I muft alfo add the hither end of our noble metropolis.

When this happy art of polite converfing fhall be thoroughly improved, good company will be no longer peftered with dull, dry, tedious ftory-tellers, nor brangling difputers: for a right fcholar of either fex in our fcience will perpetually interrupt them with fome fudden furprizing piece of wit, that fhall engage all the company in a loud laugh; and if after a paufe the grave companion refumes his thread in the following manner, *Well, but to go on with my ftory,* new interruptions come from the left and the right, till he is forced to give over.

I have likewife made fome few effays toward *felling of bargains,* as well for inftructing thofe who delight in that accomplifhment, as in compliance with my female friends at court. However I have tranfgreffed a little in this point by doing it in a manner

ner somewhat more reserved than it is now practised at St. *James*'s. At the same time, I can hardly allow this accomplishment to pass properly for a branch of that perfect polite conversation, which makes the constituent subject of my treatise, and for this I have already given my reasons. I have likewise, for further caution, left a blank in the critical point of each *bargain*, which the sagacious reader may fill up in his own mind.

As to myself, I am proud to own, that except some smattering in the *French* I am what the pedants and scholars call, a man wholly illiterate, that is to say, unlearned. But as to my own language, I shall not readily yield to many persons. I have read most of the plays, and all the miscellany poems that have been published for twenty years past. I have read Mr. *Thomas Brown*'s works entire, and had the honour to be his intimate friend, who was universally allowed to be the greatest genius of his age.

Upon what foot I stand with the present chief reigning wits, their verses recommendatory, which they have commanded

INTRODUCTION. 139

manded me to prefix before my book, will be more than a thousand witnesses: I am, and have been, likewise particularly acquainted with Mr. CHARLES GILDON, Mr. WARD, Mr. DENNIS that admirable critick and poet, and several others. Each of these eminent persons (I mean those who are still alive) have done me the honour to read this production five times over with the strictest eye of friendly severity, and proposed some, although very few amendments, which I gratefully accepted, and do here publickly return my acknowledgment for so singular a favour.

And I cannot conceal without ingratitude, the great assistance I have received from those two illustrious writers, Mr. OZELL, and captain STEVENS. These, and some others of distinguished eminence, in whose company I have passed so many agreeable hours, as they have been the great refiners of our language, so it hath been my chief ambition to imitate them. Let the POPES, the GAYS, the ARBUTHNOTS, the YOUNGS, and the rest of that snarling brood burst with envy at the praises

praises we receive from the court and kingdom.

But to return from this digression.

The reader will find, that the following collection of polite expressions will easily incorporate with all subjects of genteel and fashionable life. Those which are proper for morning-tea will be equally useful at the same entertainment in the afternoon, even in the same company, only by shifting the several questions, answers, and replies into different hands; and such as are adapted to meals will indifferently serve for dinners or suppers, only distinguishing between day-light and candle-light. By this method no diligent person of a tolerable memory can ever be at a loss.

It hath been my constant opinion, that every man, who is entrusted by nature with any useful talent of the mind, is bound by all the ties of honour, and that justice which we all owe our country, to propose to himself some one illustrious action to be performed in his life for the publick emolument: and I freely confess that so grand, so important an enterprize

INTRODUCTION.

as I have undertaken, and executed to the beſt of my power, well deſerved a much abler hand, as well as a liberal encouragement from the crown. However, I am bound ſo far to acquit myſelf, as to declare, that I have often and moſt earneſtly intreated ſeveral of my above-named friends, univerſally allowed to be of the firſt rank in wit and politeneſs, that they would undertake a work ſo honourable to themſelves, and ſo beneficial to the kingdom; but ſo great was their modeſty, that they all thought fit to excuſe themſelves, and impoſe the taſk on me, yet in ſo obliging a manner, and attended with ſuch compliments on my poor qualifications, that I dare not repeat. And, at laſt their intreaties, or rather their commands, added to that inviolable love I bear to the land of my nativity, prevailed upon me to engage in ſo bold an attempt.

I may venture to affirm without the leaſt violation of modeſty, that there is no man now alive, who hath by many degrees ſo juſt pretenſions as myſelf to the higheſt encouragement from the *crown*, the *parliament*, and the *ministry*, towards bringing this work to its due perfection. I have been assured, that several great heroes of antiquity were worshipped as gods upon the merit of having civilized a fierce and barbarous people. It is manifest I could have no other intentions, and, I dare appeal to my very enemies, if such a treatise as mine had been published some years ago, and with as much success as I am confident this will meet, I mean, by turning the thoughts of the whole nobility and gentry to the study and practice of polite conversation; whether such mean stupid writers as the *Craftsman* and his abettors could have been able to corrupt the principles of so many hundred thousand subjects, as, to the shame and grief of every whiggish, loyal, and true protestant heart, it is too manifest they have done. For I desire the honest judicious reader to make one remark, That, after having exhausted the whole * *in sickly pay-day* (if I may so

* This word is spelt by *Latinists*, *Encyclopædia*; but the judicious author wisely prefers the polite reading before the pedantick.

INTRODUCTION. 143

call it) of politeness and refinement, and faithfully digested it into the following dialogues, there cannot be found one expression relating to politicks; that the *ministry* is never mentioned, nor the word *king* above twice or thrice, and then only to the honour of his majesty; so very cautious were our wiser ancestors in forming rules for conversation as never to give offence to crowned heads, nor interfere with party disputes in the state. And indeed, although there seems to be a close resemblance between the two words *politeness* and *politicks*, yet no ideas are more inconsistent in their natures. However, to avoid all appearance of disaffection, I have taken care to enforce loyalty by an invincible argument, drawn from the very fountain of this noble science, in the following short terms, that ought to be writ in gold, *Must is for the king*; which uncontroulable maxim I took particular care of introducing in the first page of my book, thereby to instil early the best protestant loyal notions into the minds of my readers. Neither is it merely my own private opinion, that politeness is the firmest foun-

foundation upon which loyalty can be supported: for thus happily sings the divine Mr. *Tibbalds*, or *Theobalds*, in one of his birth-day poems:

I am no schollard, but I am polite:
Therefore be sure I am no Jacobite.

Hear likewise to the same purpose that great master of the whole poetick choir, our most illustrious laureat Mr. COLLY CIBBER.

Who in his talk can't speak a polite thing,
Will never loyal be to GEORGE *our king.*

I could produce many more shining passages out of our principal poets of both sexes to confirm this momentous truth. From whence I think it may be fairly concluded, that whoever can most contribute towards propagating the science contained in the following sheets thro' the kingdoms of *Great-Britain* and *Ireland*, may justly demand all the favour that the wisest court and most judicious senate are able to confer on the most deserving subject. I leave the application to my readers.

This

INTRODUCTION.

This is the work, which I have been so hardy to attempt, and without the least mercenary view. Neither do I doubt of succeeding to my full wish, except among the *Tories* and their abettors, who being all *Jacobites*, and consequently *papists* in their hearts, from a want of true taste, or by strong affectation, may perhaps resolve not to read my book, chusing rather to deny themselves the pleasure and honour of shining in polite company among the principal genius's of both sexes throughout the kingdom, than adorn their minds with this noble art; and probably apprehending (as, I confess nothing is more likely to happen) that a true spirit of loyalty to the protestant succession should steal in along with it.

If my favourable and gentle readers could possibly conceive the perpetual watchings, the numberless toils, the frequent risings in the night to set down several ingenious sentences, that I suddenly or accidentally recollected; and which, without my utmost vigilance, had been irrecoverably lost for ever: if they would consider with what incredible diligence

I daily and nightly attended at those houses where persons of both sexes, and of the most distinguished merit, used to meet and display their talents; with what attention I listened to all their discourses, the better to retain them in my memory; and then at proper seasons withdrew unobserved to enter them in my table-book, while the company little suspected what a noble work I had then in embryo: I say, if all these were known to the world, I think it would be no great presumption in me to expect, at a proper juncture, the publick thanks of both houses of parliament for the service and honour I have done to the whole nation by my single pen.

Although I have never been once charged with the least tincture of vanity, the reader will, I hope, give me leave to put an easy question: What is become of all the King of *Sweden*'s victories? where are the fruits of them at this day; or, of what benefit will they be to posterity? Were not many of his greatest actions owing, at least in part, to fortune; were not all of them owing to the valour of his troops,

troops, as much as to his own conduct? Could he have conquered the *Polish* king, or the Czar of *Muscovy* with his single arm? Far be it from me to envy or lessen the fame he hath acquired; but, at the same time I will venture to say, without breach of modesty, that I, who have alone with this right-hand subdued barbarism, rudeness, and rusticity; who have established and fixed for ever the whole system of all true politeness and refinement in conversation, should think myself most inhumanely treated by my countrymen, and would accordingly resent it as the highest indignity, to be put on a level in point of fame in after-ages with CHARLES the Twelfth late king of *Sweden*.

And yet, so incurable is the love of detraction, perhaps beyond what the charitable reader will easily believe, that I have been assured by more than one credible person, how some of my enemies have industriously whispered about, that one ISAAC NEWTON, an instrument-maker, formerly living near *Leicester-fields*, and afterwards a workman in the Mint at the *Tower*, might possibly pretend

tend to vye with me for fame in future times. The man it seems was knighted for making sun-dials better than others of his trade, and was thought to be a conjurer, because he knew how to draw lines and circles upon a slate, which nobody could understand. But, adieu to all noble attempts for endless renown, if the ghost of an obscure mechanick shall be raised up to enter into competition with me, only for his skill in making pothooks and hangers with a pencil, which many thousand accomplished gentlemen and ladies can perform as well with pen and ink upon a piece of paper, and in a manner as little intelligible as those of Sir Isaac.

My most ingenious friend already mentioned, Mr. COLLEY CIBBER, who does so much honour to the laurel crown he deservedly wears (as he hath often done to many imperial diadems placed on his head) was pleased to tell me, that if my treatise were shaped into a comedy, the representation performed to advantage on our theatre, might very much contribute to the spreading of polite conversation among

INTRODUCTION.

mong all persons of distinction through the whole kingdom.

I own the thought was ingenious, and my friend's intention good: but I cannot agree to his proposal; for Mr. CIBBER himself allowed, that the subjects handled in my work being so numerous and extensive, it would be absolutely impossible for one, two, or even six comedies to contain them. From whence it will follow, that many admirable and essential rules for polite conversation must be omitted.

And here let me do justice to my friend Mr. TIBBALDS, who plainly confessed before Mr. CIBBER himself, that such a project, as it would be a great diminution to my honour, so it would intolerably mangle my scheme, and thereby destroy the principal end at which I aimed, to form a complete body or system of this most useful science in all its parts. And therefore Mr. TIBBALDS, whose judgment was never disputed, chose rather to fall in with my proposal mentioned before of erecting publick schools and seminaries all over the kingdom to instruct the young people

people of both sexes in this art according to my rules, and in the method that I have laid down.

I shall conclude this long, but necessary introduction with a request, or indeed rather a just and reasonable demand from all lords, ladies, and gentlemen, that while they are entertaining and improving each other with those polite questions, answers, repartees, replies, and rejoinders, which I have with infinite labour, and close application during the space of thirty-six years been collecting for their service and improvement, they shall, as an instance of gratitude, on every proper occasion quote my name after this or the like manner: *Madam, as our master* WAGSTAFF *says. My Lord, as our friend* WAGSTAFF *has it.* I do likewise expect, that all my pupils shall drink my health every day at dinner and supper during my life; and that they, or their posterity shall continue the same ceremony to my *not inglorious memory*, after my decease, for ever.

A COMPLEAT
COLLECTION
OF
POLITE and INGENIOUS
CONVERSATION.
IN SEVERAL DIALOGUES.

The MEN.	The LADIES.
Lord Sparkish.	*Lady* Smart.
Lord Smart.	*Miss* Notable.
Sir John Linger.	*Lady* Answerall.
Mr. Neverout.	
Col. Atwitt.	

ARGUMENT.

Lord Sparkish *and Colonel* Atwitt *meet in the morning upon the* Mall: *Mr.* Neverout *joins them; they all go to breakfast at Lady* Smart's. *Their conversation over their tea: after which they part; but my lord and the two gentlemen are invited to dinner. Sir* John Linger *invited likewise, and comes a little too late. The whole conversation at dinner: after which the ladies retire to their tea. The conversation of the ladies without the men, who are supposed to stay and drink a bottle; but in some time, go to the ladies and drink tea with them. The conversation there. After which a party at Quadrille until three in the morning; but no conversation set down. They all take leave, and go home.*

Polite

Polite Conversation, *etc.**

St. JAMES's PARK.

Lord Sparkish *meeting Col.* Atwit.

Col. WELL met, my lord.
 Ld. Sparkish. Thank ye, Colonel. A parson would have said, I hope we shall meet in heaven. When did you see *Tom Neverout?*

Col. He's just coming towards us. Talk of the devil ----

Neverout *comes up.*

Col. How do you do, *Tom?*
Neverout. Never the better for you.
Col. I hope you're never the worse: but pray where's your manners? don't you see my Lord *Sparkish?*

---

* " I retired hither for the publick good, having two great works in hand; one to reduce the whole politeness, wit, humour, and style of *England* into a short system for the use of all persons of quality, and particularly the maids of honour,*etc.*" *Letters to and from D.* Swift, at the end of Mr. *Pope*'s works, letter liv.

Neverout. My Lord, I beg your lordſhip's pardon.

Ld. Sparkiſh. *Tom,* how is it, that you can't ſee the wood for trees? What wind blew you hither?

Neverout. Why, my Lord, it is an ill wind blows no body good; for it gives me the honour of ſeeing your lordſhip.

Col. Tom, you muſt go with us to Lady *Smart*'s to breakfaſt.

Neverout. Muſt! why Colonel, muſt's for the king.

[*Col. offering in jeſt to draw his ſword.*
Col. Have you ſpoke with all your friends?

Neverout. Colonel, as you're ſtout, be merciful.

Ld. Sparkiſh. Come, agree, agree; the law's coſtly.

[*Col. taking his hand from his hilt.*
Col. Well, *Tom,* you are never the worſe man to be afraid of me. Come along.

Neverout. What do you think I was born in a wood, to be afraid of an owl? I'll wait on you. I hope Miſs *Notable* will

DIALOGUE I. 155

will be there; egad she's very handsome, and has wit at will.

Col. Why every one as they like, as the good woman said when she kiss'd her cow.

Lord Smart's *house; they knock at the door; the* Porter *comes out.*

Lord Sparkish. Pray, are you the porter?

Porter. Yes, for want of a better.

Ld. Sparkish. Is your lady at home?

Porter. She was at home just now; but she's not gone out yet.

Neverout. I warrant this rogue's tongue is well hung.

Lady Smart's *antichamber.*

Lady Smart, *Lady* Answerall, *and Miss* Notable *at the tea-table.*

Lady Smart. My Lord, your lordship's most humble servant.

Ld. Sparkish. Madam, you spoke too late; I was your ladyship's before.

Lady Smart. O! Colonel, are you here?

Col.

Col. As sure as you're there, Madam.

Lady Smart. Oh, Mr. *Neverout!* What such a man alive!

Neverout. Ay, madam, alive, and alive like to be, at your ladyship's service.

Lady Smart. Well, I'll get a knife, and nick it down that Mr. *Neverout* came to our house. And pray what news, Mr. *Neverout?*

Neverout. Why, madam, Queen *Elizabeth's* dead.

Lady Smart. Well: Mr. *Neverout,* I see you are no changeling.

Miss Notable *comes in.*

Neverout. Miss, your slave: I hope your early rising will do you no harm. I find you are but just come out of the cloth market.

Miss. I always rise at eleven, whether it be day or no.

Col Miss, I hope you are up for all day.

Miss. Yes, if I don't get a fall before night.

Col. Miss, I heard you were out of order; pray how are you now?

Miss.

DIALOGUE I.

Miss. Pretty well, Colonel, I thank you.

Col. Pretty and well, Miss! that's two very good things.

Miss. I mean I am better than I was.

Neverout. Why then, 'tis well you were sick.

Miss. What! Mr. *Neverout*, you take me up before I'm down.

Lady Smart. Come let us leave off children's play, and go to push-pin.

Miss. [*To Lady Smart.*] Pray, madam, give me some more sugar to my tea.

Col. Oh! Miss, you must needs be very good-humour'd, you love sweet things so well.

Neverout. Stir it up with the spoon, Miss; for the deeper the sweeter.

Lady Smart. I assure you, Miss, the colonel has made you a great compliment.

Miss. I am sorry for it; for I have heard say, complimenting is lying.

Lady Smart. [*To Ld Sparkish*] My Lord, methinks the sight of you is good for sore eyes; if we had known of your coming,

coming, we would have ſtrown ruſhes for you: how has your lordſhip done this long time?

Col. Faith, Madam, he's better in health than in good conditions.

Ld Sparkiſh. Well; I ſee there's no worſe friend than one brings from home with one; and I am not the firſt man has carried a rod to whip himſelf.

Neverout. Here's poor Miſs has not a word to throw at a dog. Come, a penny for your thoughts.

Miſs. It is not worth a farthing; for I was thinking of you.

Col. riſing up.

Lady Smart. Colonel, where are you going ſo ſoon? I hope you did not come to fetch fire.

Col. Madam, I muſt needs go home for half an hour.

Miſs. Why, Colonel, they ſay, the devil's at home.

Lady Anſw. Well, but ſit while you ſtay, 'tis as cheap ſitting as ſtanding.

Col. No, madam, while I'm ſtanding I'm going.

Miſs.

DIALOGUE I.

Miss. Nay, let him go; I promise him we won't tear his cloaths to hold him.

Lady Smart. I suppose, Colonel, we keep you from better company, I mean only as to myself.

Col. Madam, I am all obedience.

Col. sits down.

Lady Smart. Lord, Miss, how can you drink your tea so hot? sure your mouth's pav'd.

How do you like this tea, Colonel?

Col. Well enough, Madam; but methinks it is a little more-ish.

Lady Smart. Oh Colonel! I understand you. *Betty* bring the canister: I have but very little of this tea left; but I don't love to make two wants of one; want when I have it, and want when I have it not. He, he, he, he. [*Laughs.*

Lady Answ. [*to the maid*] Why, sure, *Betty*, you are bewitched, the cream is burnt to.

Betty. Why, Madam, the bishop has set his foot in it.

Lady Smart. Go, run girl, and warm some fresh cream.

Betty.

Betty. Indeed, Madam, there's none left; for the cat has eaten it all.

Lady Smart. I doubt it was a cat with two legs.

Miss. Colonel, don't you love bread and butter with your tea?

Col. Yes, in a morning, Miss: for they say, butter is gold in a morning, silver at noon, but it is lead at night.

Neverout. Miss, the weather is so hot, that my butter melts on my bread.

Lady Answ. Why, butter, I've heard 'em say, is mad twice a year.

Ld Sparkish. [*to the maid*] Mrs. *Betty*, how does your body politick?

Col. Fie, my Lord, you'll make Mrs. *Betty* blush.

Lady Smart. Blush! ay, blush like a blue dog.

Neverout. Pray, Mrs. *Betty*, are you not *Tom Johnson*'s daughter?

Betty. So my mother tells me, Sir.

Ld. Sparkish. But, Mrs. *Betty*, I hear you are in love.

Betty. My Lord, I thank God, I hate nobody; I am in charity with all the world.

Lady

DIALOGUE I.

Lady Smart. Why, wench, I think thy tongue runs upon wheels this morning: how came you by that scratch upon your nose? have you been fighting with the cats?

Col. [*to miss.*] Miss, when will you be married?

Miss. One of these odd-come-shortly's, Colonel.

Neverout. Yes; they say the match is half made, the spark is willing, but miss is not.

Miss. I suppose the gentleman has got his own consent for it.

Lady Answ. Pray, my Lord, did you walk through the Park in the rain?

Ld. Sparkish. Yes, madam, we were neither sugar nor salt, we were not afraid the rain would melt us. He, he, he.
[*Laugh.*

Col. It rain'd, and the sun shone at the same time.

Neverout. Why, then the devil was beating his wife behind the door with a shoulder of mutton. [*Laugh.*

Col. A blind man would be glad to see that.

Lady Smart. Mr. *Neverout,* methinks you stand in your own light.

Neverout. Ah! Madam, I have done so all my life.

Ld. Sparkish. I'm sure he sits in mine: Prithee, *Tom,* sit a little farther: I believe your father was no glasier.

Lady Smart. Miss, dear Girl, fill me out a dish of tea, for I'm very lazy.

Miss fills a dish of tea, sweetens it, and then tastes it.

Lady Smart. What, miss, will you be my taster?

Miss. No, madam; but they say 'tis an ill cook that can't lick her own fingers.

Neverout. Pray Miss fill me another.

Miss. Will you have it now, or stay till you get it?

Lady Answ. But, colonel, they say you went to court last night very drunk: nay, I'm told for certain, you had been among the *Philistines:* no wonder the cat wink'd, when both her eyes were out.

Col. Indeed, Madam, that's a lye.

Lady Answ. 'Tis better I should lye than

DIALOGUE I.

than you fhould lofe your good manners: befides, I don't lie, I fit.

Neverout. O faith, Colonel, you muft own you had a drop in your eye: when I left you, you were half feas over.

Ld. Sparkifh. Well, I fear Lady *Anfwerall* can't live long, fhe has fo much wit.

Neverout. No; fhe can't live, that's certain; but fhe may linger thirty or forty years.

Mifs. Live long! ay, longer than a cat or a dog, or a better thing.

Lady Anfw. Oh! mifs, you muft give your vardi too!

Ld. Sparkifh. Mifs, fhall I fill you another difh of tea?

Mifs. Indeed, my lord, I have drank enough.

Ld. Sparkifh. Come, it will do you more good than a month's fafting; here take it.

Mifs. No, I thank your lordfhip; enough's as good as a feaft.

Ld. Sparkifh. Well; but if you always fay no, you'll never be married.

Lady Anſw. Do, my lord, give her a diſh; for, they ſay, maids will ſay no and take it.

Ld. Sparkiſh. Well; and I dare ſay, miſs is a maid in thought, word, and deed.

Neverout. I would not take my oath of that.

Miſs. Pray, Sir, ſpeak for yourſelf.

Lady Smart. Fie Miſs; they ſay maids ſhould be ſeen, and not heard.

Lady Anſw. Good miſs, ſtir the fire, that the tea-kettle may boil.---You have done it very well; now it burns purely. Well, miſs, you'll have a chearful huſband.

Miſs. Indeed, your ladyſhip could have ſtirred it much better.

Lady Anſw. I know that very well, huſſy; but I won't keep a dog and bark myſelf.

Neverout. What! you are ſick, miſs.

Miſs. Not at all; for her ladyſhip meant you.

Neverout. Oh! faith, miſs, you are in lob's-pound; get out as you can.

Miſs. I won't quarrel with my bread and

and butter for all that; I know when I'm well.

Lady Anſw. Well; but miſs ---

Neverout. Ah! dear madam, let the matter fall; take pity on poor miſs; don't throw water on a drowned rat.

Miſs. Indeed, Mr. *Neverout*, you ſhould be cut for the ſimples this morning: ſay a word more and you had as good eat your nails.

Ld. Sparkiſh. Pray, miſs, will you be ſo good as to favour us with a ſong?

Miſs. Indeed, my lord, I can't; for I have a great cold.

Col. Oh! Miſs, they ſay all good ſingers have colds.

Ld Sparkiſh. Pray, madam, does not miſs ſing very well?

Lady Anſw. She ſings, as one may *ſay*, my lord.

Miſs. I hear Mr. *Neverout* has a very good voice.

Col. Yes, *Tom* ſings well, but his luck's naught.

Neverout. Faith, colonel, you hit yourſelf a deviliſh box on the ear.

Col. Miſs, will you take a pinch of ſnuff.

Miſs. No, colonel, you muſt know that I never take ſnuff but when I'm angry.

Lady Anſw. Yes, yes, ſhe can take ſnuff, but ſhe has never a box to put it in.

Miſs. Pray, colonel, let me ſee that box.

Col. Madam, there's never a C upon it.

Miſs. May be there is, colonel.

Col. Ay, but May-Bees don't fly now, miſs.

Neverout. Colonel, why ſo hard upon poor miſs? Don't ſet your wit againſt a child; miſs, give me a blow, and I'll beat him.

Miſs. So ſhe pray'd me to tell you.

Ld. Sparkiſh. Pray, my lady *Smart*, what kin are you to lord *Pozz*?

Lady Smart. Why, his grandmother and mine had four elbows.

Lady Anſw. Well, methinks here's a ſilent meeting. Come, miſs, hold up your head, girl; there's money bid for you.

[*Miſs ſtarts.*

Miſs. Lord, madam, you frighten me out of my ſeven ſenſes!

Ld.

DIALOGUE I.

Ld. Sparkish. Well, I must be going.

Lady Answ. I have seen hastier people than you stay all night.

Col. [*to Lady Smart.*] *Tom Neverout* and I are to leap to-morrow for a guinea.

Miss. I believe, colonel, Mr. *Neverout* can leap at a crust better than you.

Neverout. Miss, your tongue runs before your wit; nothing can tame you but a husband.

Miss. Peace! I think I hear the church clock.

Neverout. Why you know, as the fool thinks ---

Lady Smart. Mr. *Neverout*, your handkerchief's fallen.

Miss. Let him set his foot on it, that it may'nt fly in his face.

Neverout. Well, miss ---

Miss. Ay, ay! many a one says well that thinks ill.

Neverout. Well, miss, I'll think on this.

Miss. That's rhime, if you take it in time.

Neverout. What! I see you are a poet.

Miss. Yes; if I had but the wit to shew it.

Neverout. Miss, will you be so kind as to fill me a dish of tea.

Miss. Pray let your betters be serv'd before you; I'm just going to fill one for myself; and, you know, the parson always christens his own child first.

Neverout. But I saw you fill one just now for the colonel: well, I find kissing goes by favour.

Miss. But pray, Mr. *Neverout,* what lady was that you were talking with in the side-box last *Tuesday?*

Neverout. Miss, can you keep a secret?

Miss. Yes, I can.

Neverout. Well, miss, and so can I.

Col. Odd-so! I have cut my thumb with this cursed knife!

Lady Answ. Ay; that was your mother's fault, because she only warn'd you not to cut your fingers.

Lady Smart. No, no; 'tis only fools cut their fingers, but wise folks cut their thumbs.---

Miss. I'm sorry for it, but I can't cry.

Col. Don't you think miss is grown?

Lady Answ. Ay, ill weeds grow apace.

A

DIALOGUE I.

A puff of smoke comes down the chimney.

Lady Answ. Lord, madam, does your ladyship's chimney smoke?

Col. No, madam; but they say smoke always pursues the fair, and your ladyship sat nearest.

Lady Smart. Madam, do you love Bohea tea?

Lady Answ. Why, madam, I must confess I do love it, but it does not love me.

Miss [*to lady Smart.*] Indeed, madam, your ladyship is very sparing of your tea: I protest, the last I took was no more than water bewitch'd.

Col. Pray, miss, if I may be so bold, what lover gave you that fine etuy?

Miss. Don't you know? then keep counsel.

Lady Answ. I'll tell you, colonel, who gave it her; it was the best lover she will ever have while she lives, her own dear papa.

Neverout. Methinks, miss, I don't much like the colour of that ribbon.

Miss.

Miss. Why then, Mr. *Neverout*, do you see, if you don't much like it, you may look off of it.

Ld. Sparkish. I don't doubt, madam, but your ladyship has heard that Sir *John Brisk* has got an employment at court.

Lady Smart. Yes, yes; and I warrant he thinks himself no small fool now.

Neverout. Yet, madam, I have heard some people take him for a wise man.

Lady Smart. Ay, ay; some are wise, and some are otherwise.

Lady Answ. Do you know him, Mr. *Neverout?*

Neverout. Know him! ay, as well as the beggar knows his dish.

Col. Well; I can only say that he has better luck than honester folks: but pray, how came he to get this employment?

Ld. Sparkish. Why, by chance, as the man kill'd the devil.

Neverout. Why, miss, you are in a brown study; what's the matter? methinks you look like mum-chance, that was hang'd for saying nothing.

Miss. I'd have you to know, I scorn your words.

Never-

DIALOGUE I.

Neverout. Well; but fcornful dogs will eat dirty puddings.

Mifs. Well; my comfort is, your tongue is no flander. What! you would not have one be always on the high grin.

Neverout. Cry map-fticks, madam; no offence I hope.

[*Lady* Smart *breaks a tea-cup.*

Lady Anfw. Lord, madam, how came you to break your cup.

Lady Smart. I can't help it, if I would cry my eyes out.

Mifs. Why fell it, madam, and buy a new one with fome of the money.

Col. 'Tis a folly to cry for fpilt milk.

Lady Smart. Why, if things did not break or wear out, how would tradefmen live?

Mifs. Well; I am very fick, if any body car'd for it.

Neverout. Come, then, mifs, e'en make a die of it, and then we fhall have a burying of our own.

Mifs. The devil take you, *Neverout*, befides all fmall curfes.

Lady Anfw. Marry come up, what,
plain

plain *Neverout!* methinks you might have an M under your girdle, mifs.

Lady Smart. Well, well, naught's never in danger; I warrant, mifs will fpit in her hand, and hold faft. Colonel, do you like this bifket?

Col. I'm like all fools; I love every thing that's good.

Lady Smart. Well, and isn't it pure good?

Col. 'Tis better than a worfe.

Footman brings the colonel a letter.

Lady Anfw. I fuppofe, colonel, that's a billet-doux from your miftrefs.

Col. Egad, I don't know whence it comes; but whoe'er writ it, writes a hand like a foot.

Mifs. Well, you may make a fecret of it, but we can fpell, and put together.

Neverout. Mifs, what fpells b double uzzard?

Mifs. Buzzard in your teeth, Mr. *Neverout.*

Lady Smart. Now you are up, Mr. *Neverout,* will you do me the favour, to
do

DIALOGUE I.

do me the kindnefs, to take off the tea-kettle?

Ld Sparkifh. I wonder what makes thefe bells ring.

Lady Anfw. Why, my lord, I fuppofe, becaufe they pull the ropes.

[*Here all laugh.*

Neverout *plays with a tea-cup.*

Mifs. Now a child would have cried half an hour before it would have found out fuch a pretty play-thing.

Lady Smart. Well faid, mifs: I vow, Mr. *Neverout*, the girl is too hard for you.

Neverout. Ay, mifs will fay any thing but her prayers, and thofe fhe whiftles.

Mifs. Pray, colonel, make me a prefent of that pretty penknife.

Ld Sparkifh. Ay, mifs, catch him at that and hang him.

Col. Not for the world, dear mifs; it will cut love.

Ld. Sparkifh. Colonel, you fhall be married firft, I was juft going to fay that.

Lady Smart. Well, but for all that, I can tell who is a great admirer of mifs: pray, mifs, how do you like Mr. *Spruce?*

I fwear

I swear I have often seen him cast a sheep's eye out of a calf's head at you: deny it if you can.

Miss. Oh! madam; all the world knows that Mr. *Spruce* is a general lover.

Col. Come, miss, 'tis too true to make a jest on. [*Miss blushes.*

Lady Answ. Well, however, blushing is some sign of grace.

Neverout. Miss says nothing; but I warrant she pays it off with thinking.

Miss. Well, ladies and gentlemen, you are pleas'd to divert yourselves; but, as I hope to be sav'd, there's nothing in it.

Lady Smart. Touch a gall'd horse, and he'll wince: love will creep where it dare not go: I'd hold a hundred pound Mr. *Neverout* was the inventor of that story; and, colonel, I doubt you had a finger in the pye.

Lady Answ. But, colonel, you forgot to salute miss when you came in; she said you had not been here a long time.

Miss. Fie, madam! I vow, colonel, I said no such thing; I wonder at your ladyship!

Col. Miss, I beg your pardon ---
Goes

DIALOGUE I.

Goes to salute her, she struggles a little.

Miss. Well, I'd rather give a knave a kiss for once than be troubled with him; but, upon my word, you are more bold than welcome.

Lady Smart. Fie, fie, miss! for shame of the world, and speech of good people.

Neverout to Miss, *who is cooking her tea and bread and butter.*

Neverout. Come, come, miss, make much of naught; good folks are scarce.

Miss. What! and you must come in with your two eggs a penny, and three of them rotten.

Col. [*to Ld. Sparkish.*] But, my lord, I forgot to ask you, how you like my new cloaths?

Ld. Sparkish. Why, very well, colonel; only, to deal plainly with you, methinks the worst piece is in the middle.

[*Here a loud laugh, often repeated.*

Col. My lord, you are too severe on your friends.

Miss. Mr. *Neverout*, I'm hot, are you a sot?

Neverout. Miss, I'm cold, are you a scold? take you that. *Lady*

Lady Smart. I confess that was home. I find, Mr. *Neverout*, you won't give your head for the washing, as they say.

Miss. Oh! he's a sore man where the skin's off. I see Mr. *Neverout* has a mind to sharpen the edge of his wit on the whetstone of my ignorance.

Ld. Sparkish. Faith, *Tom*, you are struck! I never heard a better thing.

Neverout. Pray, miss, give me leave to scratch you for that fine speech.

Miss. Pox on your picture, it cost me a groat the drawing.

Neverout [*to Lady Smart.*] 'Sbuds, madam, I have burnt my hand with your plaguy tea-kettle.

Lady Smart. Why, then, Mr. *Neverout*, you must say, God save the king.

Neverout. Did you ever see the like?

Miss. Never but once, at a wedding.

Col. Pray, miss, how old are you?

Miss. Why, I'm as old as my tongue, and a little older than my teeth.

Ld. Sparkish. [*to Lady Answ.*] Pray, madam, is miss *Buxom* married? I hear 'tis all over the town.

Lady

DIALOGUE I.

Lady Anſw. My lord, ſhe's either married, or worſe.

Col. If ſhe be'nt married, at leaſt ſhe's luſtily promis'd. But, is it certain that Sir *John Blunderbuſs* is dead at laſt?

Ld. Sparkiſh. Yes, or elſe he's ſadly wrong'd, for they have buried him.

Miſs. Why, if he be dead, he'll eat no more bread.

Col. But, is he really dead?

Lady Anſw. Yes, colonel, as ſure as you're alive ----

Col. They ſay he was an honeſt man.

Lady Anſw. Yes, with good looking to.

Miſs *feels a pimple on her face.*

Miſs. Lord! I think my goodneſs is coming out. Madam, will your ladyſhip pleaſe to lend me a patch?

Neverout. Miſs, if you are a maid, put your hand upon your ſpot.

Miſs. --- There ---

Covering her face with both her hands.

Lady Smart. Well, thou art a mad girl. [*Gives her a tap.*

Miſs

Miss. Lord, Madam, is that a blow to give a child?

Lady Smart *lets fall her handkerchief, and the colonel stoops for it.*

Lady Smart. Colonel, you shall have a better office.

Col. Oh, madam, I can't have a better than to serve your ladyship.

Col. [*to Lady Sparkish*] Madam, has your ladyship read the new play, written by a lord? it is call'd *Love in a hollow tree.*

Lady Sparkish. No, colonel.

Col. Why, then your ladyship has one pleasure to come.

Miss *sighs.*

Neverout. Pray, miss, why do you sigh?

Miss. To make a fool ask, and you are the first.

Neverout. Why, miss, I find there is nothing but a bit and a blow with you.

Lady Answ. Why, you must know, miss is in love.

Miss. I wish, my head may never ake till that day.

Ld.

DIALOGUE I.

Ld. Sparkish. Come miss, never sigh, but send for him.

[*Lady* Smart *and Lady* Answerall *speaking together.*
If he be hang'd, he'll come hopping, and if he be drown'd, he'll come dropping.

Miss. Well, I swear you'll make one die with laughing.

Miss *plays with a tea-cup, and* Neverout *plays with another.*

Neverout. Well; I see, one fool makes many.

Miss. And you are the greatest fool of any.

Neverout. Pray, miss, will you be so kind to tie this string for me with your fair hands? it will go all in your day's work.

Miss. Marry, come up, indeed; tie it yourself, you have as many hands as I; your man's man will have a fine office truly: come, pray stand out of my spitting-place.

Neverout. Well; but miss, don't be angry.

Miss. No; I was never angry in my

life but once, and then no body car'd for it, fo I refolv'd never to be angry again.

Neverout. Well; but if you'll tie it, you fhall never know what I'll do for you.

Mifs. So I fuppofe, truly.

Neverout. Well; but I'll make you a fine prefent one of thefe days.

Mifs. Ay; when the devil's blind, and his eyes are not fore yet.

Neverout. No, mifs, I'll fend it you to-morrow.

Mifs. Well, well: to-morrow's a new day; but I fuppofe, you mean to-morrow come never.

Neverout. Oh! 'tis the prettieft thing: I affure you, there came but two of them over in three fhips.

Mifs. Would I could fee it, quoth blind *Hugh.* But why did you not bring me a prefent of fnuff this morning?

Neverout. Becaufe, mifs, you never afk'd me; and 'tis an ill dog, that's not worth whiftling for.

Ld. Sparkifh [*to Lady Anfw.*] Pray, madam, how came your ladyfhip laft Thur-

DIALOGUE I.

Thurſday to go to that odious puppet-ſhow?

Col. Why, to be ſure, her ladyſhip went to ſee, and to be ſeen.

Lady Anſw. You have made a fine ſpeech, colonel: pray, what will you take for your mouth-piece?

Ld. Sparkiſh. Take that, colonel: but, pray, madam, was my lady *Snuff* there? They ſay ſhe's extremely handſome.

Lady Smart. They muſt not ſee with my eyes, that think ſo.

Neverout. She may paſs muſter well enough.

Lady Anſw. Pray how old do you take her to be?

Col. Why, about five or ſix and twenty.

Miſs. I ſwear ſhe's no chicken; ſhe's on the wrong ſide of thirty, if ſhe be a day.

Lady Anſw. Depend upon it, ſhe'll never ſee five and thirty, and a bit to ſpare.

Col. Why they ſay, ſhe's one of the chief toaſts in town.

Lady Smart. Ay, when all the reſt are out of it.

Miſs.

Miss. Well; I woud'nt be as sick as she's proud for all the world.

Lady Answ. She looks, as if butter woud'nt melt in her mouth, but I warrant, cheese won't choak her. I hear my lord What d'ye call him is courting her.

Ld. Sparkish. What lord d'ye mean, *Tom?*

Miss. Why, my lord, I suppose Mr. *Neverout* means the lord of the Lord knows what.

Col. They say she dances very fine.

Lady Answ. She did; but I doubt her dancing days are over.

Col. I can't pardon her for her rudeness to me.

Lady Smart. Well; but you must forget and forgive.

Footman *comes in.*

Lady Smart. Did you call *Betty?*
Footman. She's coming, madam.
Lady Smart. Coming! ay, so is *Christ-mas.*

Betty *comes in.*

Lady Smart. Come, get ready my things. Where has the wench been these three hours? *Betty.*

DIALOGUE I.

Betty. Madam, I can't go faster, than my legs will carry me.

Lady Smart. Ay, thou hast a head, and so has a pin. But, my lord, all the town has it, that Miss *Caper* is to be married to Sir *Peter Giball*; one thing is certain, that she hath promis'd to have him.

Ld. Sparkish. Why madam, you know, promises are either broken or kept.

Lady Answ. I beg your pardon, my lord; promises and pye-crust are made to be broken.

Lady Smart. Nay, I had it from my lady *Carry-lye*'s own mouth. I tell you my tale and my tale's author; if it be a lye, you had it as cheap as I.

Lady Answ. She and I had some words last *Sunday* at church; but I think I gave her her own.

Lady Smart. Her tongue runs like the clapper of a mill; she talks enough for herself and all the company.

Neverout. And yet she simpers like a firmity-kettle.

Miss *looking in a glass.*

Miss. Lord, how my head is drest to-day!

Col. Oh, madam! a good face needs no band.

Miss. No; and a bad one deserves none.

Col. Pray, miss, where is your old acquaintance Mrs. *Wayward?*

Miss. Why, where should she be; you must needs know; she's in her skin.

Col. I can answer that: what if you were as far out as she's in? ---

Miss. Well, I promis'd to go this evening to *Hyde-Park* on the water; but I protest I'm half afraid.

Neverout. Never fear, miss; you have the old proverb on your side, Naught's ne'er in danger.

Col. Why, miss, let *Tom Neverout* wait on you; and then I warrant, you'll be as safe as a thief in a mill; for you know, He that's born to be hang'd, will never be drowned.

Neverout. Thank you, colonel, for your good

good word; but faith, if ever I hang, it ſhall be about a fair lady's neck.

Lady Smart. Who's there? Bid the children be quiet, and not laugh ſo loud.

Lady Anſw. Oh, madam, let 'em laugh, they'll ne'er laugh younger.

Neverout. Miſs, I'll tell you a ſecret, if you'll promiſe never to tell it again.

Miſs. No, to be ſure; I'll tell it to nobody but friends and ſtrangers.

Neverout. Why then, there's ſome dirt in my tea-cup.

Miſs. Come, come, the more there's in't, the more there's on't.

Lady Anſw. Poh! you muſt eat a peck of dirt before you die.

Col. Ay, ay; it goes all one way.

Neverout. Pray, miſs, what's a clock?

Miſs. Why, you muſt know, 'tis a thing like a bell, and you are a fool that can't tell.

Neverout. [*to Lady Anſw.*] Pray, madam, do you tell me; for I have let my watch run down.

Lady Anſw. Why, 'tis half an hour paſt hanging-time.

Col.

Col. Well; I'm like the butcher that was looking for his knife, and had it in his mouth: I have been ſearching my pockets for my ſnuff-box, and, egad, here it is in my hand.

Miſs. If it had been a bear, it would have bit you, colonel: well, I wiſh I had ſuch a ſnuff-box.

Neverout. You'll be long enough before you wiſh your ſkin full of eyelet-holes.

* *Col.* Wiſh in one hand ---

Miſs. Out upon you: Lord, what can the man mean?

Ld. Sparkiſh. This tea's very hot.

Lady Anſw. Why, it came from a hot place, my lord.

Colonel *ſpills his tea.*

Lady Smart. That's as well done, as if I had done it myſelf.

Col. Madam, I find you live by ill neighbours, when you are forc'd to praiſe yourſelf.

---

* This ſentence is remarkably characteriſtic and beautiful; by the firſt it appears that miſs knew the reſt, and by the latter, that in the ſame breath ſhe laboured to conceal her knowledge.

Lady

Lady Smart. So they pray'd me to tell you.

Neverout. Well, I won't drink a drop more; if I do, twill go down like chopt hay.

Miss. Pray don't say no, till you are afk'd.

Neverout. Well, what you pleafe, and the reft again.

Mifs *ftooping for a pin.*

Miss. I have heard 'em fay, that a pin a day is a groat a year. Well, as I hope to be married, forgive me for fwearing, I vow 'tis a needle.

Col. Oh! the wonderful works of nature, that a black hen fhould lay a white egg!

Neverout. What! you have found a mare's neft, and laugh at the eggs?

Miss. Pray keep your breath to cool your porridge.

Neverout. Mifs, there was a very pleafant accident laft night at St. *James's* Park.

Miss. [*to Lady Smart.*] What was it your ladyfhip was going to fay juft now?

Neverout. Well, miss; tell a mare a tale.---

Miss. I find you love to hear yourself talk.

Neverout. Why, if you won't hear my tale, kiss my, *etc.*

Miss. Out upon you for a filthy creature!

Neverout. What, miss! must I tell you a story, and find you ears?

Ld. Sparkish [*to Lady Smart.*] Pray, madam, don't you think Mrs. *Spendall* very genteel?

Lady Smart. Why, my lord, I think she was cut out for a gentlewoman, but she was spoil'd in the making: she wears her cloaths as if they were thrown on her with a pitch-fork; and, for the fashion, I believe they were made in the reign of Queen BESS.

Neverout. Well, that's neither here nor there; for you know, the more careless the more modish.

Col. Well, I'd hold a wager there will be a match between her and *Dick Dolt*: and I belie e I can see as far into a millstone as another man.

Miss.

DIALOGUE I.

Miſs. Colonel, I muſt beg your pardon a thouſand times; but they ſay, an old ape has an old eye.

Neverout. Miſs, what do you mean! you'll ſpoil the colonel's marriage, if you call him old.

Col. Not ſo old, nor yet ſo cold---You know the reſt miſs.

Miſs. Manners is a fine thing, truly.

Col. Faith, miſs, depend upon it, I'll give you as good as you bring: what! if you give a jeſt, you muſt take a jeſt.

Lady Smart. Well, Mr. *Neverout*, you'll ne'er have done till you break that knife, and then the man won't take it again.

Miſs. Why, madam, fools will be meddling; I wiſh he may cut his fingers. I hope you can ſee your own blood without fainting.

Neverout. Why, miſs, you ſhine this morning like a ſh---n barn-door: you'll never hold out at this rate; pray ſave a little wit for to-morrow.

Miſs. Well, you have ſaid your ſay; if people will be rude, I have done; my
comfort

comfort is, 'twill be all one a thousand year hence.

Neverout. Miss, you have shot your bolt: I find you must have the last word --- Well, I'll go to the opera to-night --- No, I can't neither, for I have some business---and yet I think I must; for I promis'd to squire the countess to her box.

Miss. The countess of *Puddledock*, I suppose.

Neverout. Peace, or war, miss?

Lady Smart. Well, Mr. *Neverout*, you'll never be mad, you are of so many minds.

As Miss *rises, the chair falls behind her.*

Miss Well; I shan't be lady-mayoress this year.

Neverout. No, miss, 'tis worse than that; you won't be married this year.

Miss. Lord! you make me laugh, tho' I an't well.

Neverout, *as* Miss *is standing, pulls her suddenly on his lap.*

Neverout. Now, colonel, come, sit down

DIALOGUE I.

down on my lap; more facks upon the mill.

Mifs. Let me go? ar'n't you forry for my heavinefs?

Neverout. No, mifs; you are very light; but I don't fay you are a light huffy. Pray take up the chair for your pains.

Mifs. 'Tis but one body's labour, you may do it yourfelf; I wifh you would be quiet, you have more tricks than a dancing bear.

Neverout *rifes to take up the chair, and* Mifs *fits in his.*

Neverout. You wou'dn't be fo foon in my grave, madam.

Mifs. Lord! I have torn my petticoat with your odious romping; my rents are coming in; I'm afraid I fhall fall into the ragman's hands.

Neverout. I'll mend it, mifs.

Mifs. You mend it! go, teach your grannam to fuck eggs.

Neverout. Why, mifs, you are fo crofs, I could find in my heart to hate you.

Mifs.

Miss. With all my heart; there will be no love loft between us.

Neverout. But pray, my lady *Smart*, does not miss look as if she could eat me without salt?

Miss. I'll make you one day sup sorrow for this.

Neverout. Well, follow your own way, you'll live the longer.

Miss. See, madam, how well I have mended it.

Lady Smart. 'Tis indifferent, as *Doll* danc'd.

Neverout. 'Twill last as many nights as days.

Miss. Well, I knew I should never have your good word.

Lady Smart. My lord, my lady *Answerall* and I was walking in the Park last night till near eleven; 'twas a very fine night.

Neverout. Egad, so was I; and I'll tell you a comical accident; egad, I lost my understanding.

Miss. I'm glad you had any to lose.

Lady Smart. Well, but what do you mean?

Ne--

DIALOGUE I.

Neverout. Egad, I kick'd my foot against a stone, and tore off the heel of my shoe, and was forc'd to limp to a cobler in the *Pall Mall* to have it put on. He, he, he, he. [*All laugh.*

Col. Oh! 'twas a delicate night to run away with another man's wife.

Neverout *sneezes.*

Miss. God bless you, if you han't taken snuff.

Neverout. Why, what if I have, miss?

Miss. Why then, the duce take you.

Neverout. Miss, I want that diamond ring of yours.

Miss. Why then, want's like to be your master.

Neverout *looking at the ring.*

Neverout. Ay, marry, this is not only, but also; where did you get it?

Miss. Why, where 'twas to be had; where the devil got the friar.

Neverout. Well; if I had such a fine diamond ring, I woud'nt stay a day in *England:* but you know, far-fetch'd and dear-bought is fit for ladies. I warrant, this cost your father two-pence half-penny.

Miss sitting between Neverout *and the* Colonel.

Miss. Well; here's a rose between two nettles.

Neverout. No, madam; with submission, here's a nettle between two roses.

Colonel *stretching himself.*

Lady Smart. Why, colonel, you break the king's laws; you stretch without a halter.

Lady Answ. Colonel, some ladies of your acquaintance have promis'd to breakfast with you, and I am to wait on them; what will you give us?

Col. Why, faith, madam, batchelors fare; bread and cheese and kisses.

Lady Answ. Poh! what have you batchelors to do with your money, but to treat the ladies? you have nothing to keep, but your own four quarters.

Lady Smart. My lord, has captain *Brag* the honour to be related to your lordship?

Ld. Sparkish. Very nearly, madam; he's my cousin-german quite remov'd.

DIALOGUE I.

Lady Anſw. Pray is he not rich?

Ld. Sparkiſh. Ay, a rich rogue, two ſhirts and a rag.

Col. Well, however, they ſay he has a great eſtate, but only the right owner keeps him out of it.

Lady Smart. What religion is he of?

Ld. Sparkiſh. Why he is an *Anything-arian.*

Lady Anſw. I believe he has his religion to chuſe, my lord.

Neverout *ſcratches his head.*

Miſs. Fie, Mr. *Neverout*, ar'n't you aſham'd! I beg pardon for the expreſſion, but I'm afraid your boſom-friends are become your back-biters.

Neverout. Well, miſs, I ſaw a flea once on your pinner, and a louſe is a man's companion, but a flea is a dog's companion: however, I wiſh you would ſcratch my neck with your pretty white hand.

Miſs. And who would be fool then? I woud'n't touch a man's fleſh for the univerſe. You have the wrong ſow by the ear, I aſſure you; that's meat for your maſter.

Neverout. Miſs *Notable*, all quarrels laid aſide, pray ſtep hither for a moment.

Miſs. I'll waſh my hands and wait on you, ſir; but pray come hither, and try to open this lock.

Neverout. We'll try what we can do.

Miſs. We! --- what have you pigs in your belly.

Neverout. Miſs, I aſſure you, I am very handy at all things.

Miſs. Marry, hang them that can't give themſelves a good word: I believe you may have an even hand to throw a louſe in the fire.

Col. Well, I muſt be plain; here's a very bad ſmell.

Miſs. Perhaps, colonel, the fox is the finder.

Neverout, No, colonel; 'tis only your teeth againſt rain: but ---

Miſs. Colonel, I find you would make a very bad poor man's ſow.

Colonel *coughing.*

Col. I have got a ſad cold.

Lady Anſw. Ay; 'tis well if one can get any thing theſe hard times.

Miſs. [*To Col.*] Choak, chicken, there's more a hatching.   *Lady*

DIALOGUE I.

Lady Smart. Pray, colonel, how did you get that cold?

Ld. Sparkish. Why, madam, I suppose the colonel got it by lying a bed barefoot.

Lady Answ. Why then, colonel, you must take it for better for worse, as a man takes his wife.

Col. Well, ladies, I apprehend you without a constable.

Miss. Mr. *Neverout!* Mr. *Neverout!* come hither this moment.

Lady Smart. [*imitating her*] Mr. *Neverout!* Mr. *Neverout!* I wish he were tied to your girdle.

Neverout. What's the matter! whose mare's dead now?

Miss. Take your labour for your pains; you may go back again, like a fool as you came.

Neverout. Well, miss, if you deceive me a second time, 'tis my fault.

Lady Smart. Colonel, methinks your coat is too short.

Col. It will be long enough before I get another, madam.

Miſs. Come, come; the coat's a good coat, and come of good friends.

Neverout. Ladies, you are miſtaken in the ſtuff; 'tis half ſilk.

Col. Tom Neverout, you are a fool, and that's your fault.

A great noiſe below.

Lady Smart. Hey! what a clattering is here! one would think hell was broke looſe.

Miſs. Indeed, madam, I muſt take my leave, for I a'n't well.

Lady Smart. What! you are ſick of the mulligrubs with eating chopt hay?

Miſs. No, indeed, madam; I'm ſick and hungry, more need of a cook than a doctor.

Lady Anſw. Poor miſs! ſhe's ſick as a cuſhion, ſhe wants nothing but ſtuffing.

Col. If you are ſick, you ſhall have a caucle of calf's eggs.

Neverout. I can't find my gloves.

Miſs. I ſaw the dog running away with ſome dirty thing a while ago.

Col. Miſs, you have got my handkerchief; pray, let me have it.

Lady

DIALOGUE I.

Lady Smart. No; keep it miſs; for they ſay, poſſeſſion is eleven points of the law.

Miſs. Madam, he ſhall ne'er have it again; 'tis in huckſters hands

Lady Anſw. What! I ſee 'tis raining again.

Ld. Sparkiſh. Why, then, madam, we muſt do as they do in *Spain*.

Miſs. Pray, my lord, how is that?

Ld. Sparkiſh. Why, madam, we muſt let it rain.

Miſs *whiſpers Lady* Smart.

Neverout. There's no whiſpering, but there's lying

Miſs. Lord! Mr. *Neverout*, you are as pert as a pear-monger this morning.

Neverout. Indeed, miſs, you are very handſome.

Miſs. Poh! I know that already; tell me news.

Somebody knocks at the door.

Footman *comes in.*

Footman [*to Col.*] An pleaſe your honour,

nour, there's a man below wants to speak to you.

Col. Ladies, your pardon for a minute.
[*Col. goes out.*

Lady Smart. Miss, I sent yesterday to know how you did, but you were gone abroad early.

Miss. Why, indeed, madam, I was hunch'd up in a hackney-coach with three country acquaintance, who call'd upon me to take the air as far as *High-gate.*

Lady Smart. And had you a pleasant airing?

Miss. No, madam; it rain'd all the time; I was jolted to death, and the road was so bad, that I scream'd every moment, and call'd to the coachman, pray, friend, don't spill us.

Neverout, So, miss, you were afraid, that pride wou'd have a fall.

Miss. Mr. *Neverout,* when I want a fool, I'll send for you.

Ld. Sparkish. Miss, did'n't your left ear burn last night?

Miss. Pray why, my lord?

Ld. Sparkish. Because I was then in
some

DIALOGUE I.

some company where you were extoll'd to the skies, I assure you.

Miss My lord, that was more their goodness than my desert.

Ld. Sparkish. They said, that you were a compleat beauty.

Miss. My lord, I am as God made me.

Lady Smart. The girl's well enough, if she had but another nose.

Miss. Oh! madam, I know I shall always have your good word; you love to help a lame dog over the stile.

One knocks.

Lady Smart. Who's there? you're on the wrong side of the door; come in, if you be fat.

Colonel comes in again.

Ld. Sparkish. Why, colonel, you are a man of great business.

Col. Ay, ay, my lord, I'm like my lord-mayor's fool, full of business, and nothing to do.

Lady Smart. My lord, don't you think the colonel's mightily fall'n away of late?

Ld.

Ld Sparkish. Ay, fall'n from a horse-load to a cart-load.

Col. Why, my lord, egad I am like a rabbit, fat and lean in four and twenty hours.

Lady Smart. I assure you, the colonel walks as strait as a pin.

Miss. Yes; he's a handsome-body'd man in the face.

Neverout. A handsome foot and leg: God-a-mercy shoe and stocking!

Col. What! three upon one! that's foul play: this would make a parson swear.

Neverout. Why, miss, what's the matter? you look as if you had neither won nor lost.

Col. Why, you must know, miss lives upon love.

Miss. Yes, upon love and lumps of the cupboard.

Lady Answ. Ay; they say love and peas-porridge are two dangerous things; one breaks the heart, and the other the belly.

Miss. [*imitating Lady* Answerall's *tone*] Very

Very pretty! one breaks the heart, and the other the belly.

Lady Answ. Have a care; they say, mocking is catching.

Miss. I never heard that.

Neverout. Why, then, miss, you have a wrinkle --- more than ever you had before.

Miss. Well; live and learn.

Neverout. Ay; and be hang'd, and forget all.

Miss. Well, Mr. *Neverout*, take it as you please; but I swear, you are a saucy jack to use such expressions.

Neverout. Why then, miss, if you go to that, I must tell you there's ne'er a jack but there's a jill.

Miss. Oh! Mr. *Neverout*, every body knows that you are the pink of courtesy.

Neverout. And, miss, all the world allows, that you are the flower of civility.

Lady Smart. Miss, I hear there was a great deal of company where you visited last night: pray, who were they?

Miss. Why, there was old lady *Forward*, miss *To-and-again*, Sir *John Ogle*, my lady *Clapper*, and I, quoth the dog.

Col.

Col. Was your visit long, miss?

Miss. Why, truly, they went all to the opera; and so poor Pilgarlick came home alone.

Neverout. Alack a-day, poor miss! methinks it grieves me to pity you.

Miss. What! you think, you said a fine thing now; well, if I had a dog with no more wit, I would hang him.

Ld. Smart. Miss, if it is manners, may I ask which is oldest, you or lady *Scuttle?*

Miss. Why, my lord, when I die for age, she may quake for fear.

Lady Smart. She's a very great gadder abroad.

Lady Answ. Lord! she made me follow her last week through all the shops like a * Tantiny pig.

Lady Smart. I remember, you told me, you had been with her from *Dan* to *Bersheba.*

Colonel *spits.*

Col. Lord! I shall die; I cannot spit from me.

---

*St. *Anthony's* pig: It being fabled of Saint *Anthony* the Hermit, that he wrought a miraculous cure on an hog, it became a custom in several places to tie a bell about the neck of a pig, and maintain it at the common charge in honour to his memory. Hence the proverb, To follow like a Tantiny-pig.

DIALOGUE I.

Miss. Oh! Mr. *Neverout*, my little *Countess* has juſt litter'd; ſpeak me fair, and I'll ſet you down for a puppy.

Neverout. Why, miſs, if I ſpeak you fair, perhaps I mayn't tell truth.

Ld. Sparkiſh. Ay, but *Tom*, ſmoke that, ſhe calls you puppy by craft.

Neverout. Well, miſs, you ride the fore-horſe to-day.

Miſs. Ay, many one ſays well, that thinks ill.

Neverout. Fie, miſs; you ſaid that once before; and, you know, too much of one thing is good for nothing.

Miſs. Why, ſure, we can't ſay a good thing too often.

Ld. Sparkiſh. Well, ſo much for that, and butter for fiſh; let us call another cauſe. Pray, madam, does your ladyſhip know Mrs. *Nice?*

Lady Smart. Perfectly well, my lord; ſhe's nice by name, and nice by nature.

Ld. Sparkiſh. Is it poſſible ſhe could take that booby *Tom Blunder* for love?

Miſs. She had good ſkill in horſe-fleſh, that would chuſe a gooſe to ride on.

Lady Anfw. Why, my lord, 'twas her fate; they fay, marriage and hanging go by deftiny.

Col. I believe fhe'll never be burnt for a witch.

Ld. Sparkifh. They fay, marriages are made in heaven; but I doubt, when fhe was married, fhe had no friend there.

Neverout. Well, fhe's got out of God's blefling into the warm fun.

Col. The fellow's well enough, if he had any guts in his brains.

Lady Smart. They fay, thereby hangs a tale.

Ld. Sparkifh. Why, he's a mere hobbledehoy, neither a man nor a boy.

Mifs. Well, if I were to chufe a hufband, I would never be married to a little man.

Neverout. Pray, why fo, mifs? for they fay, of all the evils we ought to chufe the leaft.

Mifs. Becaufe folks would fay, when they faw us together, there goes the woman and her hufband.

Col. [*to Lady Smart*] Will your ladyfhip be on the *Mall* to-morrow night?

Lady

DIALOGUE I.

Lady Smart. No, that won't be proper; you know to-morrow's *Sunday.*

Ld. Sparkish. What then, madam? they say, the better day, the better deed.

Lady Answ. Pray, Mr. *Neverout,* how do you like lady *Fruzz?*

Neverout. Pox on her! she's as old as *Poles* *.

Miss. So will you be, if you ben't hang'd when you're young.

Neverout. Come, miss, let us be friends: will you go to the park this evening?

Miss. With all my heart, and a piece of my liver; but not with you.

Lady Smart. I'll tell you one thing, and that's not two; I'm afraid I shall get a fit of the head-ach to-day.

Col. Oh! madam, don't be afraid; it comes with a fright.

Miss [*to Lady Answ.*] madam, one of your ladyship's lappets is longer than t'other.

Lady Answ. Well, no matter; they that ride on a trotting horse will ne'er perceive it.

Neverout. Indeed, miss, your lappets hang worse.

* For St *Paul*'s church.

Miſs. Well, I love a lyar in my heart, and you fit me to a hair.

Miſs *riſes up.*

Neverout. Duce take you, miſs; you trod on my foot: I hope you don't intend to come to my bed-ſide.

Miſs. In troth, you are afraid of your friends, and none of them near you.

Ld. Sparkiſh. Well ſaid, girl! [*giving her a chuck*] take that; they ſay, a chuck under the chin is worth two kiſſes.

Lady Anſw. But, Mr. *Neverout*, I wonder why ſuch a handſome, ſtrait, young gentleman as you, don't get ſome rich widow.

Ld. Sparkiſh. Strait! ay, ſtrait as my leg, and that's crooked at knee.

Neverout. Faith, Madam, if it rain'd rich widows, none of them would fall upon me. Egad, I was born under a threepenny planet, never to be worth a groat.

Lady Anſw. No, Mr. *Neverout*; I believe you were born with a caul on your head; you are ſuch a favourite among the ladies: but what think you of widow *Prim?* ſhe's immenſely rich.

DIALOGUE I.

Neverout. Hang her! they say her father was a baker.

Lady Smart. Ay; but it is not, what is she, but what has she, now-a-days.

Col. Tom, faith, put on a bold face for once, and have at the widow. I'll speak a good word for you to her.

Lady Answ. Ay; I warrant, you'll speak one word for him, and two for yourself.

Miss. Well; I had that at my tongue's end.

Lady Answ. Why, miss, they say, good wits jump.

Neverout. Faith, madam, I had rather marry a woman I lov'd, in her smock, than widow *Prim*, if she had her weight in gold.

Lady Smart. Come, come, Mr. *Neverout*, marriage is honourable, but housekeeping is a shrew.

Lady Answ. Consider, Mr. *Neverout*, four bare legs in a bed; and you are a younger brother.

Col. Well, madam; the younger brother is the better gentleman: however, *Tom*, I would advise you to look before you leap.

Ld. Sparkish. The colonel says true; besides, you can't expect to wive and thrive in the same year.

Miss. [*shuddering.*] Lord! there's somebody walking over my grave.

Col. Pray, lady *Answerall*, where was you last *Wednesday*, when I did myself the honour to wait on you? I think your ladyship is one of the tribe of *Gad*.

Lady Answ. Why, colonel, I was at church.

Col. Nay, then will I be hang'd, and my horse too.

Neverout. I believe her ladyship was at a church with a chimney in it.

Miss. Lord, my petticoat! how it hangs by jommetry!

Neverout. Perhaps the fault may be in your shape.

Miss. [*looking gravely*] Come, Mr. *Neverout*, there's no jest like the true jest; but, I suppose you think my back's broad enough to bear every thing.

Neverout. Madam, I humbly beg your pardon.

Miss. Well, sir, your pardon's granted.

Neverout. Well, all things have an end,

end, and a pudden has two, up up on me my-my word. [*ſtutters.*

Miſs. What! Mr. *Neverout*, can't you ſpeak without a ſpoon?

Ld. Sparkiſh. [*to Lady Smart*] Has your ladyſhip ſeen the ducheſs ſince your falling out?

Lady Smart. Never, my lord, but once at a viſit; and ſhe look'd at me as the devil look'd over *Lincoln*.

Neverout. Pray, miſs, take a pinch of my ſnuff.

Miſs. What! you break my head, and give me a plaiſter; well, with all my heart; once, and not uſe it.

Neverout. Well, miſs; if you wanted me and your victuals, you'd want your two beſt friends.

Col. [*to Neverout.*] *Tom,* miſs and you muſt kiſs and be friends.

Neverout *ſalutes* Miſs.

Miſs. Any thing for a quiet life: my noſe itch'd, and I knew I ſhould drink wine, or kiſs a fool.

Col. Well, *Tom,* if that ben't fair, hang fair.

Neverout. I never said a rude thing to a lady in my life.

Miss. Here's a pin for that lye; I'm sure lyars had need have good memories. Pray, colonel, was not he very uncivil to me but just now?

Lady Answ. Mr. *Neverout*, if miss will be angry for nothing, take my counsel, and bid her turn the buckle of her girdle behind her.

Neverout. Come, lady *Answerall*, I know better things; miss and I are good friends; don't put tricks upon travellers.

Col. Tom, Not a word of the pudden, I beg you.

Lady Smart. Ah, colonel! you'll never be good, nor then neither.

Ld. Sparkish. Which of the good's d'ye mean? good for something, or good for nothing?

Miss. I have a blister on my tongue; yet I don't remember, I told a lye.

Lady Answ. I thought you did just now.

Ld. Sparkish. Pray, madam, what did thought do?

Lady Answ. Well, for my life, I cannot conceive what your lordship means.

Ld.

DIALOGUE I.

Ld. Sparkiſh. Indeed, madam, I meant no harm.

Lady Smart. No, to be ſure, my lord! you are as innocent as a devil of two years old.

Neverout. Madam, they ſay, ill doers are ill deemers; but I don't apply it to your ladyſhip.

Miſs *mending a hole in her lace.*

Miſs. Well, you ſee, I'm mending; I hope I ſhall be good in time; look, lady *Anſwerall*, is it not well mended?

Lady Anſw. Ay, this is ſomething like a tanſy.

Neverout. Faith, miſs, you have mended it, as a tinker mends a kettle; ſtop one hole, and make two.

Lady Smart. Pray, colonel, are you not very much tann'd?

Col. Yes, madam; but a cup of *Chriſtmas* ale will ſoon waſh it off.

Ld. Sparkiſh. Lady *Smart*, does not your ladyſhip think Mrs. *Fade* is mightily alter'd ſince her marriage?

Lady Anſw. Why, my lord, ſhe was handſome in her time; but ſhe cannot eat

eat her cake and have her cake: I hear she's grown a mere otomy.

Lady Smart. Poor creature! the black ox has set his foot upon her already.

Miss. Ay; she has quite lost the blue on the plumb.

Lady Smart. And yet, they say, her husband is very fond of her still.

Lady Answ. Oh! madam; if she would eat gold, he would give it her.

Neverout. [*to Lady Smart*] madam, have you heard, that lady *Queasy* was lately at the playhouse *incog?*

Lady Smart. What! lady *Queasy* of all women in the world! Do you say it upon Rep?

Neverout. Poz, I saw her with my own eyes; she sat among the mob in the gallery; her own ugly fiz: and she saw me look at her.

Col. Her ladyship was plaguily bamb'd; I warrant it put her into the hipps.

Neverout. I smoked her huge nose, and, egad, she put me in mind of the woodcock, that strives to hide his long bill, and then thinks nobody sees him.

Col.

Col. Tom, I advise you, hold your tongue; for you'll never say so good a thing again.

Lady Smart. Miss, what are you looking for?

Miss. Oh! madam; I have lost the finest needle ---

Lady Answ. Why, seek till you find it, and then you won't lose your labour.

Neverout. The loop of my hat is broke; how shall I mend it? [*he fastens it with a pin*] Well, hang him, say I, that has no shift.

Miss. Ay, and hang him that has one too many.

Neverout. Oh! miss; I have heard a sad story of you.

Miss. I defy you, Mr. *Neverout*; nobody can say, black's my eye.

Neverout. I believe, you wish they could.

Miss. Well; but who was your author? Come, tell truth, and shame the devil.

Neverout. Come then, miss; guess who it was that told me; come, put on your considering-cap.

Miss. Well, who was it?

Neverout. Why, one that lives within a mile of an oak.

Miss. Well, go hang yourself in your own garters; for I'm sure, the gallows groans for you.

Neverout. Pretty miss! I was but in jest.

Miss. Well, but don't let that stick in your gizzard.

Col. My lord, does your lordship know Mrs. *Talkall?*

Ld. Sparkish. Only by sight; but I hear she has a great deal of wit; and egad, as the saying is, mettle to the back.

Lady Smart. So I hear.

Col. Why *Dick Lubber* said to her t'other day, madam, you can't cry bo to a goose: yes, but I can, said she; and, egad, cry'd bo full in his face. We all thought we should break our hearts with laughing.

Ld. Sparkish. That was cutting with a vengeance: And prithee how did the fool look?

Col. Look! egad, he look'd for all the world like an owl in an ivy-bush.

DIALOGUE I.

A child comes in screaming.

Miss. Well, if that child was mine, I'd whip it till the blood came; peace, you little vixen! if I were near you, I would not be far from you.

Lady Smart. Ay, ay; batchelors wives and maids children are finely tutor'd.

Lady Answ. Come to me, master; and I'll give you a sugar-plumb. Why, miss, you forget that ever you was a child yourself. [*She gives the child a lump of sugar.*] I have heard 'em say, boys will long.

Col. My lord, I suppose you know that Mr. *Buzzard* has married again?

Lady Smart. This is his fourth wife; then he has been shod round.

Col. Why, you must know, she had a month's mind to *Dick Frontless,* and thought to run away with him; but her parents forc'd her to take the old fellow for a good settlement.

Ld. Sparkish. So the man got his mare again.

Ld. Smart. I'm told he said a very good thing to *Dick*; said he, You think us old fellows are fools; but we old fellows know young fellows are fools.

Col. I know nothing of that; but I know, he's devilish old, and she's very young.

Lady Anfw. Why, they call that a match of the world's making.

Mifs. What if he had been young, and she old?

Neverout. Why, mifs, that would have been a match of the devil's making; but when both are young, that's a match of God's making.

Mifs fearching her pockets for a thimble, brings out a nutmeg.

Neverout. Oh! mifs, have a care; for if you carry a nutmeg in your pocket, you'll certainly be married to an old man.

Mifs. Well, and if I ever be married, it shall be to an old man; they always make the beft hufbands; and it is better to be an old man's darling, than a young man's warling.

Neverout. Faith, mifs, if you fpeak as you think, I'll give you my mother for a maid.

Lady

DIALOGUE I.

Lady Smart *rings the bell.*

Footman *comes in.*

Lady Smart. Harkee, you fellow; run to my lady *Match*, and defire fhe will remember to be here at fix, to play at quadrille: d'ye hear, if you fall by the way, don't ftay to get up again.

Footman. Madam, I don't know the houfe.

Lady Smart. That's not for want of ignorance; follow your nofe; go, enquire among the fervants.

Footman *goes out, and leaves the door open.*

Lady Smart. Here, come back, you fellow; why did you leave the door open? Remember, that a good fervant muft always come when he's call'd, do what he's bid, and fhut the door after him.

The Footman *goes out again, and falls down ftairs.*

Lady Anfw. Neck or nothing; come down,

down, or I'll fetch you down: well, but I hope the poor fellow has not sav'd the hangman a labour.

Neverout. Pray, madam, smoke miss yonder biting her lips, and playing with her fan.

Miss. Who's that takes my name in vain?

She runs up to them, and falls down.

Lady Smart. What, more falling! do you intend the frolick should go round?

Lady Answ. Why, miss, I wish you may not have broke her ladyship's floor.

Neverout. Miss, come to me, and I'll take you up.

Lady Sparkish. Well, but without a jest, I hope, miss, you are not hurt.

Col. Nay, she must be hurt for certain; for you see her head is all of a lump.

Miss. Well, remember this, colonel, when I have money, and you have none.

Lady Smart. But, colonel, when do you design to get a house, and a wife, and a fire to put her in.

Miss. Lord! who would be married to a soldier, and carry his knapsack?

DIALOGUE I.

Neverout. Oh, madam: *Mars* and *Venus*, you know.

Col. Egad, madam, I'd marry to-morrow, if I thought I could bury my wife juft when the honey-moon is over; but they fay, a woman has as many lives as a cat.

Lady Anfw. I find, the colonel thinks, a dead wife under the table is the beft goods in a man's houfe.

Lady Smart. O but, colonel, if you had a good wife, it would break your heart to part with her.

Col. Yes, madam; for they fay, he that has loft his wife and fixpence, has loft a tefter.

Lady Smart. But, colonel, they fay, that every married man fhould believe there's but one good wife in the world, and that's his own.

Col. For all that, I doubt, a good wife muft be befpoke; for there's none ready made.

Mifs. I fuppofe, the gentleman s a woman-hater; but, fir, I think you ought to remember, that you had a mother: and pray, if it had not been for a woman,

man, where would you have been, colonel?

Col. Nay, miſs, you cry'd whore firſt, when you talk'd of the knapſack.

Lady Anſw. But I hope you won't blame the whole ſex, becauſe ſome are bad.

Neverout. And they ſay, he that hates woman, fuck'd a ſow.

Col. Oh! madam; there's no general rule without an exception.

Lady Smart. Then, why don't you marry, and ſettle?

Col. Egad, madam, there's nothing will ſettle me but a bullet.

Ld. Sparkiſh. Well, colonel, there's one comfort, that you need not fear a cannon-bullet.

Col. Why ſo, my lord?

Ld. Sparkiſh. Becauſe they ſay, he was curs'd in his mother's belly, that was kill'd by a cannon-bullet.

Miſs. I ſuppoſe, the colonel was croſs'd in his firſt love, which makes him ſo ſevere on all the ſex.

Lady Anſw. Yes; and I'll hold a hundred to one, that the colonel has been

over

over head and ears in love with some lady that has made his heart ake.

Col. Oh! madam, we soldiers are admirers of all the fair sex.

Miss. I wish I could see the colonel in love till he was ready to die.

Lady Smart. Ay; but I doubt, few people die for love in these days.

Neverout. Well, I confess, I differ from the colonel; for I hope to have a rich and a handsome wife yet before I die.

Col. Ay, *Tom*; live horse, and thou shalt have grass.

Miss. Well, colonel; but whatever you say against women, they are better creatures than men; for men were made of clay, but woman was made of man.

Col. Miss, you may say what you please; but, faith, you'll never lead apes in hell.

Neverout. No, no; I'll be sworn miss has not an inch of nun's flesh about her.

Miss. I understumble you, gentlemen.

Neverout. Madam, your humble-cum-dumble.

Ld. Sparkish. Pray, miss, when did you

you see your old acquaintance Mrs. *Cloudy?* you and she are two, I hear.

Miss. See her! marry, I don't care whether I ever see her again; God bless my eye-sight.

Lady Answ. Lord! why she and you were as great as two inkle-weavers. I've seen her hug you as the devil hugg'd the witch.

Miss. That's true; but I'm told for certain, she's no better than she should be.

Lady Smart. Well, God mend us all; but you must allow, the world is very censorious; I never heard that she was a naughty pack.

Col. [*to Neverout*] Come, sir *Thomas* when the king pleases, when do you intend to march?

Ld. Sparkish. Have patience. *Tom*, is your friend *Ned Rattle* married?

Neverout. Yes, faith, my lord; he has tied a knot with his tongue, that he can never untie with his teeth.

Lady Smart. Ay; marry in haste, and repent at leisure.

Lady

Lady Anſw. Has he got a good fortune with his lady? for they ſay, something has ſome favour, but nothing has no flavour.

Neverout. Faith, madam, all he gets by her, he may put into his eye and ſee never the worſe.

Miſs. Then, I believe, he heartily wiſhes her in *Abraham*'s boſom.

Col. Pray, my lord, how does *Charles Limber* and his fine wife agree?

Ld. Sparkiſh. Why, they ſay, he's the greateſt cuckold in town.

Neverout. Oh! but my lord, you ſhould always except my lord-mayor.

Miſs. Mr. *Neverout!*

Neverout. Hay, madam, did you call me?

Miſs. Hay; why hay is for horſes.

Neverout. Why, miſs, then you may kiſs —

Col. Pray, my lord, what's a clock by your oracle?

Ld. Sparkiſh. Faith, I can't tell, I think my watch runs upon wheels.

Neverout. Miſs, pray be ſo kind to call

call a servant to bring me a glass of small beer: I know you are at home here.

Miss. Every fool can do as they're bid: Make a page of your own age, and do it yourself.

Neverout. Chuse, proud fool; I did but ask you.

Miss *puts her hand upon her knee.*

Neverout. What! miss, are you thinking of your sweet-heart? is your garter slipping down?

Miss. Pray, Mr. *Neverout,* keep your breath to cool your porridge; you measure my corn by your bushel.

Neverout. Indeed, miss, you lye ---

Miss. Did you ever hear any thing so rude.

Neverout. I mean, you lye ---- under a mistake.

Miss. If a thousand lyes could choak you, you would have been choaked many a day ago

Miss *strives to snatch* Neverout's *snuff-box.*

Neverout. Madam, you missed that, as you miss'd your mother's blessing.

She

DIALOGUE I.

She tries again, and miffes.

Neverout. Snap ſhort makes you look ſo lean, miſs.

Miſs. Poh! you are ſo robuſtious, you had like to put out my eye; I aſſure you, if you blind me, you muſt lead me.

Lady Smart. Dear miſs be quiet; and bring me a pincuſhion out of that cloſet.

Miſs *opens the cloſet-door, and ſqualls.*

Lady Smart. Lord bleſs the girl! what's the matter now?

Miſs. I vow, madam, I ſaw ſomething in black; I thought it was a ſpirit.

Col. Why miſs, did you ever ſee a ſpirit?

Miſs. No, ſir; I thank God, I never ſaw any thing worſe than myſelf.

Neverout. Well, I did a very fooliſh thing yeſterday, and was a great puppy for my pains.

Miſs. Very likely; for they ſay, many a true word's ſpoke in jeſt.

Footman *returns.*

Lady Smart. Well, did you deliver your

your Meſſage? you are fit to be ſent for ſorrow, you ſtay ſo long by the way.

Footman. Madam, my Lady was not at home, ſo I did not leave the Meſſage.

Lady Smart. This it is to ſend a fool of an errand.

Ld. Sparkiſh. [*looking at his watch*] 'Tis paſt twelve a clock.

Lady Smart. Well, what is that among all us?

Ld. Sparkiſh. Madam, I muſt take my leave: come, gentlemen, are you for a march?

Lady Smart. Well, but your lordſhip and the colonel will dine with us to-day; and, Mr. *Neverout*, I hope, we ſhall have your good company: there will be no ſoul elſe, beſides my own lord and theſe ladies; for every body knows, I hate a croud; I would rather want vittles than elbow-room: we dine punctually at three.

Ld. Sparkiſh. Madam, we'll be ſure to attend your ladyſhip.

Col. Madam, my ſtomach ſerves me inſtead of a clock.

Ano-

DIALOGUE I.

Another Footman *comes back.*

Lady Smart. Oh! you are the t'other fellow I sent: well, have you been with my lady *Club?* you are good to send of a dead man's errand.

Footman. Madam, my lady *Club* begs your ladyship's pardon; but she is engaged to-night.

Miss. Well, Mr. *Neverout*, here's the back of my hand to you.

Neverout. Miss, I find, you will have the last word. Ladies, I am more yours than my own.

DIALOGUE II.

Lord Smart *and the former company at three o'clock coming to dine.*

After salutations.

Lord Smart.

I'M sorry I was not at home this morning, when you all did us the honour to call here: but I went to the levee to-day.

Ld. Sparkish. Oh! my lord; I'm sure the loss was ours.

Lady Smart. Gentlemen and ladies, you are come to a sad dirty house; I am sorry for it, but we have had our hands in mortar.

Ld. Sparkish. Oh! madam; your ladyship is pleas'd to say so; but I never saw any thing so clean and so fine; I profess, it is a perfect paradise.

Lady Smart. My lord, your lordship is always very obliging.

Ld. Sparkish. Pray, madam, whose picture is that?

DIALOGUE II.

Lady Smart. Why, my lord, it was drawn for me.

Ld. Sparkish. I'll swear the painter did not flatter your ladyship.

Col. My lord, the day is finely clear'd up.

Ld. Smart. Ay colonel; 'tis a pity that fair weather should ever do any harm. [*To Neverout.*] Why, *Tom*, you are high in the mode.

Neverout. My lord, it is better to be out of the world than out of the fashion.

Ld. Smart. But, *Tom*, I hear you and miss are always quarrelling: I fear, it is your fault; for I can assure you, she is very good-humour'd.

Neverout. Ay, my lord; so is the devil when he's pleas'd.

Ld. Smart. Miss, what do you think of my friend *Tom*?

Miss. My lord, I think he's not the wisest man in the world; and truly, he's sometimes very rude.

Ld. Sparkish. That may be true; but yet, he that hangs *Tom* for a fool, may find a knave in the halter.

Miss. Well, however, I wiſh he were hang'd, if it were only to try.

Neverout. Well, miſs, if I muſt be hang'd, I won't go far to chuſe my gallows; it ſhall be about your fair neck.

Miss. I'll ſee your noſe cheeſe firſt, and the dogs eating it: but, my lord, Mr. *Neverout*'s wit begins to run low; for, I vow, he ſaid this before; pray, colonel, give him a pinch, and I'll do as much for you.

Ld. Sparkiſh. My lady *Smart*, your ladyſhip has a very fine ſcarf.

Lady Smart. Yes, my lord; it will make a flaming figure in a country church.

Footman *comes in.*

Footman. Madam, dinner's upon the table.

Col. Faith, I am glad of it; my belly began to cry cupboard.

Neverout. I wiſh, I may never hear worſe news.

Miss. What! Mr. *Neverout*, you are in great haſte; I believe your belly thinks your throat is cut.

DIALOGUE II.

Neverout. No, faith, miss; three meals a day, and a good supper at night will serve my turn.

Miss. To say the truth, I'm hungry.

Neverout. And I'm angry; so let us both go fight.

They go in to dinner, and after the usual compliments, take their seats.

Lady Smart. Ladies and gentlemen, will you eat any oysters before dinner?

Col. With all my heart. [*Takes an oyster*] He was a bold man that first eat an oyster.

Lady Smart. They say, oysters are a cruel meat, because we eat them alive: then they are an uncharitable meat, for we leave nothing to the poor; and they are an ungodly meat, because we never say grace.

Neverout. Faith, that's as well said, as if I had said it myself.

Lady Smart. Well, we are well set, if we be but as well serv'd: come, colonel, handle your arms: shall I help you to some beef?

Col.

Col. If your ladyship please; and, pray, don't cut like a mother-in-law, but send me a large slice: for I love to lay a good foundation. I vow, 'tis a noble sir-loyn.

Neverout. Ay; here's cut and come again.

Miss. But pray, why is it call'd a Sir-loyn?

Ld. Smart. Why you must know, that our king *James* the First, who lov'd good eating, being invited to dinner by one of his nobles, and seeing a large loyn of beef at his table, he drew out his sword, and in a frolic knighted it. Few people know the secret of this.

Ld. Sparkish. Beef is man's meat, my lord.

Ld. Smart. But, my lord, I say, beef is the king of meat.

Miss. Pray, what have I done, that I must not have a plate?

Lady Smart. [*to Lady Answ.*] What will your ladyship please to eat?

Lady Answ. Pray, madam, help yourself.

Col.

DIALOGUE II.

Col. They say, eating and scratching wants but a beginning: if you'll give me leave, I'll help myself to a slice of this shoulder of veal.

Lady Smart. Colonel, you can't do a kinder thing: well, you are all heartily welcome, as I may say.

Col. They say there are thirty and two good bits in a shoulder of veal.

Lady Smart. Ay, colonel; thirty bad bits, and two good ones: you see, I understand you; but I hope you have got one of the two good ones.

Neverout. Colonel, I'll be of your mess.

Col. Then pray, *Tom*, carve for yourself: they say, two hands in a dish, and one in a purse: Hah! said I well, *Tom?*

Neverout. Colonel, you spoke like an oracle.

Miss. [*to Lady Answ*] Madam, will your ladyship help me to some fish?

Ld. Smart. [*to Neverout.*] *Tom*, they say fish should swim thrice.

Neverout. How is that, my lord?

Ld.

Ld. Smart. Why, *Tom*, firſt it ſhould ſwim in the ſea (do you mind me?) then it ſhould ſwim in butter; and at laſt, ſirrah, it ſhould ſwim in good claret. I think I have made it out.

Footman [*to Ld Smart.*] My lord, Sir *John Linger* is coming up.

Ld. Smart. God ſo! I invited him to dine with me to-day, and forgot it: well, deſire him to walk in.

Sir John Linger *comes in.*

Sir John. What! are you at it? why, then, I'll be gone.

Lady Smart. Sir *John*, I beg you will ſit down; come, the more the merrier.

Sir John. Ay; but the fewer the better cheer.

Lady Smart. Well, I am the worſt in the world at making apologies; it was my lord's fault: I doubt you muſt kiſs the hare's foot.

Sir John. I ſee you are faſt by the teeth.

Col. Faith, ſir *John*, we are killing that that would kill us.

DIALOGUE II.

Ld. Sparkish. You see, sir *John*, we are upon a business of life and death: come, will you do as we do? you are come in pudding-time.

Sir John. Ay; this would be doing, if I were dead. What! you keep court-hours I see: I'll be going, and get a bit of meat at my inn.

Lady Smart. Why, we won't eat you, sir *John*.

Sir John. It is my own fault; but I was kept by a fellow, who bought some *Derbyshire* oxen of me.

Neverout. You see, sir *John*, we staid for you as one horse does for another.

Lady Smart. My lord, will you help sir *John* to some beef? Lady *Answerall*, pray eat, you see your dinner: I am sure, if we had known we should have such good company, we should have been better provided; but you must take the will for the deed. I'm afraid you are invited to your loss.

Col. And pray, sir *John*, how do you like the town? you have been absent a long time.

Sir John. Why, I find little *London* ſtands juſt where it did when I left it laſt.

Neverout. What do you think of *Hanover-Square?* Why, ſir *John, London* is gone out of town ſince you ſaw it.

Lady Smart. Sir *John,* I can only ſay, you are heartily welcome; and I wiſh I had ſomething better for you.

Col. Here's no ſalt; cuckolds will run away with the meat.

Ld. Smart. Pray edge a little, to make more room for ſir *John:* ſir *John,* fall to; you know, half an hour is ſoon loſt at dinner.

Sir John. I proteſt I can't eat a bit, for I took ſhare of a beef-ſtake and two mugs of ale with my chapman, beſides a tankard of *March* beer, as ſoon as I got out of my bed.

Lady Anſw. Not freſh and faſting, I hope?

Sir John. Yes, faith, madam; I always waſh my kettle, before I put the meat in it.

Lady Smart. Poh! ſir *John,* you have ſeen nine houſes ſince you eat laſt: come, you

you have kept a corner of your ftomach for a piece of venifon-pafty.

Sir John. Well, I'll try what I can do when it comes up.

Lady Anfw. Come, fir *John*, you may go farther, and fare worfe.

Mifs. [*to Neverout.*] Pray, Mr. *Neverout*, will you pleafe to fend me a piece of tongue?

Neverout. By no means, madam; one tongue's enough for a woman.

Col. Mifs, here's a tongue, that never told a lye.

Mifs. That was, becaufe it could not fpeak. Why, colonel, I never told a lye in my life.

Neverout. I appeal to all the company, whether that be not the greateft lye that ever was told.

Col. [*to Neverout.*] Prithee, *Tom*, fend me the two legs, and rump, and liver of that pigeon; for, you muft know, I love what nobody elfe loves.

Neverout. But what if any of the ladies fhould long? Well, here take it, and the d---l do you good with it.

Lady

Lady Answ. Well; this eating and drinking takes away a body's stomach.

Neverout. I am sure I have lost mine.

Miss. What! the bottom of it, I suppose.

Neverout. No, really, miss; I have quite lost it.

Miss. I should be very sorry a poor body had found it.

Lady Smart. But, sir *John*, we hear you are married since we saw you last: what! you have stolen a wedding, it seems.

Sir John. Well; one can't do a foolish thing once in one's life, but one must hear of it a hundred times.

Col. And pray, sir *John*, how does your lady unknown?

Sir John. My wife's well, colonel, and at your service in a civil way. Ha, ha.

[*He laughs.*

Miss. Pray, sir *John*, is your lady tall or short?

Sir John. Why, miss, I thank God, she is a little evil.

Ld. Sparkish. Come, give me a glass of claret.

DIALOGUE II.

Footman *fills him a bumper.*

Ld. Sparkish. Why do you fill so much?

Neverout. My lord, he fills as he loves you.

Lady Smart. Miss, shall I send you some cowcomber?

Miss. Madam, I dare not touch it; for they say, cowcumbers are cold in the third degree.

Lady Smart. Mr. *Neverout,* do you love pudden?

Neverout. Madam, I'm like all fools, I love every thing that is good; but the proof of the pudden is in the eating.

Col. Sir *John,* I hear you are a great walker, when you are at home.

Sir John. No, faith, colonel; I always love to walk with a horse in my hand: but I have had devilish bad luck in horse-flesh of late.

Ld. Smart. Why then, Sir *John* you must kiss a parson's wife.

Lady Smart. They say, Sir *John,* that your lady has a great deal of wit.

Sir John. Madam, she can make a pudden; and has just wit enough to know her husband's breeches from another man's.

Ld Smart. My Lord *Sparkish*, I have some excellent cyder; will you please to taste it?

Ld. Sparkish. My lord, I should like it well enough, if it were not treacherous.

Ld. Smart. Pray my lord, how is it treacherous?

Ld. Sparkish. Because it smiles in my face and cuts my throat. [*Here a loud laugh*]

Miss. Odd-so! Madam; your knives are very sharp, for I have cut my finger.

Lady Smart. I am sorry for it; pray, which finger? (God bless the mark.)

Miss. Why, this finger: no, 'tis this: I vow I can't find which it is.

Neverout. Ay; the fox had a wound, and he could not tell where, *etc.* Bring some water to throw in her face.

Miss. Pray, Mr. *Neverout*, did you ever draw a sword in anger? I warrant you

you would faint at the sight of your own blood.

Lady Smart. Mr. *Neverout,* shall I send you some veal?

Neverout. No, Madam; I don't love it.

Miss. Then pray for them that do. I desire your ladyship will send me a bit.

Ld. Smart. Tom, my service to you.

Neverout. My lord, this moment I did myself the honour to drink to your lordship.

Ld. Smart. Why then that's *Hertfordshire* kindness.

Neverout. Faith, my lord, I pledged myself; for I drank twice together without thinking.

Ld. Sparkish. Why then, colonel, my humble service to you.

Neverout. Pray, my lord, don't make a bridge of my nose.

Ld. Sparkish. Well, a glass of this wine is as comfortable as matrimony to an old woman.

Col. Sir *John,* I design one of these days to come and beat up your quarters in *Derbyshire.*

Sir John. Faith, colonel, come, and welcome; and ſtay away, and heartily welcome: but you were born within the ſound of *Bow* bell, and don't care to ſtir ſo far from *London.*

Miſs. Pray, colonel, ſend me ſome fritters.

Colonel *takes them out with his hand.*

Col. Here, miſs; they ſay, fingers were made before forks, and hands before knives.

Lady Smart. Methinks this pudden is too much boil'd.

Lady Anſw. Oh! madam, they ſay a pudden is poiſon, when it is too much boil'd.

Neverout. Miſs, ſhall I help you to a pigeon? here's a pigeon ſo finely roaſted, it cries, come eat me.

Miſs. No, ſir; I thank you.

Neverout. Why, then you may chuſe.

Miſs. I have choſen already.

Neverout. Well, you may be worſe offer'd, before you are twice married.

DIALOGUE II.

The Colonel *fills a large plate of foupe.*

Ld. Smart. Why, colonel, you don't mean to eat all that foupe?

Col. O my lord, this is my fick difh; when I'm well, I'll have a bigger.

Mifs. [*to Col.*] Sup, *Simon*; very good broth.

Neverout. This feems to be a good pullet.

Mifs. I warrant, Mr. *Neverout* knows what's good for himfelf.

Ld. Sparkifh. Tom, I fhan't take your word for it; help me to a wing.

Neverout *tries to cut off a wing.*

Neverout. Egad I can't hit the joint.

Ld. Sparkifh. Why then, think of a cuckold.

Neverout. Oh! now I have nick'd it.
[*Gives it to Ld.* Sparkifh.

Ld. Sparkifh. Why, a man may eat this, though his wife lay a dying.

Col. Pray, friend, give me a glafs of fmall beer, if it be good.

Ld. Smart. Why, colonel, they fay, there is no fuch thing as good fmall beer, good brown bread, or a good old woman.

Lady Smart. [*to Lady Anfw.*] Madam, I beg your ladyſhip's pardon; I did not ſee you when I was cutting that bit.

Lady Anfw. Oh! madam; after you is good manners.

Lady Smart. Lord! here's a hair in the ſauce.

Lady Sparkiſh. Then ſet the hounds after it.

Neverout. Pray, colonel, help me however to ſome of that ſame ſauce.

Col. Come; I think you are more ſauce than pig.

Ld. Smart. Sir *John*, chear up: my ſervice to you: well, what do you think of the world to come?

Sir John. Truly, my lord, I think of it as little as I can.

Lady Smart. [*putting a ſkewer on a plate*] Here, take this ſcewer, and carry it down to the cook, to dreſs it for her own dinner.

Neverout. I beg your ladyſhip's pardon; but this ſmall beer is dead.

Lady Smart. Why, then, let it be bury'd.

Col.

DIALOGUE II.

Col. This is admirable black pudden: mifs, fhall I carve you fome? I can juft carve pudden, and that's all; I am the worft carver in the world; I fhould never make a good chaplain.

Mifs. No, thank ye, colonel; for they fay, thofe that eat black pudden will dream of the devil.

Ld. Smart. O, here comes the venifon-pafty: here, take the foupe away.

Ld. Smart. [*He cuts it up, and taftes the venifon.*] 'fbuds, this venifon is mufty.

Neverout *eats a piece, and it burns his mouth.*

Ld. Smart. What's the matter, *Tom?* you have tears in your eyes, I think: what doft cry for, man?

Neverout. My lord, I was juft thinking of my poor grandmother; fhe died juft this very day feven years.

Mifs *takes a bit, and burns her mouth.*

Neverout. And pray, mifs, why do you cry too?

Mifs. Becaufe you were not hang'd the day your grandmother died.

Ld. Smart. I'd have given forty pounds, miss, to have said that.

Col. Egad, I think the more I eat, the hungrier I am.

Ld. Sparkish. Why, colonel, they say one shoulder of mutton drives down another.

Neverout. Egad, if I were to fast for my life, I would take a good breakfast in the morning, a good dinner at noon, and a good supper at night.

Ld. Sparkish. My lord, this venison is plaguily pepper'd; your cook has a heavy hand.

Ld. Smart. My lord, I hope you are pepper-proof: come, here's a health to the founders.

Lady Smart. Ay; and to the confounders too.

Ld. Smart. Lady *Answerall*, does not your ladyship love venison?

Lady Answ. No, my lord, I can't endure it in my sight; therefore please to send me a good piece of meat and crust.

Ld. Sparkish. [*drinks to Neverout*] Come,

Come, *Tom*; not always to my friends, but once to you.

Neverout. [*drinks to Lady Smart.*] Come, madam; here's a health to our friends, and hang the reſt of our kin.

Lady Smart. [*to Lady Anſw.*] madam, will your ladyſhip have any of this hare?

Lady Anſw. No, madam; they ſay, 'tis melancholy meat.

Lady Smart. Then, madam, ſhall I ſend you the brains? I beg your ladyſhip's pardon; for they ſay, 'tis not good manners to offer brains.

Lady Anſw. No, madam; for perhaps it will make me hair-brain'd.

Neverout. Miſs, I muſt tell you one thing.

Miſs. [*with a glaſs in her hand*] Hold your tongue, Mr. *Neverout*; don't ſpeak in my tip.

Col. Well, he was an ingenious man, that firſt found out eating and drinking.

Ld. Sparkiſh. Of all vittles drink digeſts the quickeſt: give me a glaſs of wine.

Neverout. My lord, your wine is too ſtrong.

Ld. Smart. Ay, *Tom*; as much as you are too good.

Miſs. This almond pudden was pure good; but it is grown quite cold.

Neverout. So much the better, miſs; cold pudden will ſettle your love.

Miſs. Pray, Mr. *Neverout*, are you going to take a voyage?

Neverout. Why do you aſk, miſs?

Miſs. Becauſe you have laid in ſo much beef.

Sir John. You two have eat up the whole pudden betwixt you.

Miſs. Sir *John*, here's a little bit left; will you pleaſe to have it?

Sir John. No, thankee; I don't love to make a fool of my mouth.

Col. [*calling to the butler*] *John*, is your ſmall beer good?

Butler. An pleaſe your honour, my lord and lady like it; I think it is good.

Col. Why then, *John*, d'ye ſee? if you are ſure your ſmall beer is good, d'ye mark? then, give me a glaſs of wine.

[*All laugh.*

DIALOGUE II.

Colonel *tasting the wine.*

Ld. Smart. Sir *John*, how does your neighbour *Gatherall* of the *Peak?* I hear he has lately made a purchase.

Sir John. Oh, *Dick Gatherall* knows how to butter his bread as well as any man in *Darbyshire*.

Ld. Smart. Why, he us'd to go very fine, when he was here in town.

Sir John. Ay; and it became him, as a saddle becomes a sow.

Col. I know his lady, and I think she is a very good woman.

Sir John. Faith, she has more goodness in her little finger, than he has in his whole body.

Ld. Smart. Well, colonel, how do you like that wine?

Col. This wine should be eaten; it is too good to be drunk.

Ld. Smart. I'm very glad you like it; and pray don't spare it.

Col. No, my lord; I'll never starve in a cook's shop.

Ld. Smart. And pray, sir *John*, what do you say to my wine?

Sir John. I'll take another glafs firft: fecond thoughts are beft.

Ld. Sparkifh. Pray, lady *Smart,* you fit near that ham; will you pleafe to fend me a bit.

Lady Smart. With all my heart. [*She fends him a piece*] Pray, my lord, how do you like it?

Ld. Sparkifh. I think it is a limb of *Lot*'s wife. [*He eats it with muftard*] E-gad, my lord, your muftard is very uncivil.

Lady Smart. Why uncivil, my lord?

Ld. Sparkifh. Becaufe it takes me by the nofe, egad.

Lady Smart. Mr, *Neverout,* I find you are a very good carver.

Col. O madam, that is no wonder; for you muft know, *Tom Neverout* carves o' *Sundays.*

Neverout *overturns the falt-celler.*

Lady Smart. Mr. *Neverout,* you have overturn'd the falt, and that's a fign of anger: I'm afraid, mifs and you will fall out.

DIALOGUE II.

Lady Answ. No, no; throw a little of it into the fire, and all will be well.

Neverout. Oh, madam, the falling out of lovers, you know.

Miss. Lovers! very fine! fall out with him! I wonder when we were in.

Sir John. For my part, I believe the young gentlewoman is his sweetheart, there's so much fooling and fidling betwixt them: I'm sure, they say in our country, that shiddle-come sh--'s the beginning of love.

Miss. I own, I love Mr. *Neverout,* as the devil loves holy water: I love him like pye, I'd rather the devil had him than I.

Neverout. Miss, I'll tell you one thing.

Miss. Come, here's t'ye, to stop your mouth.

Neverout. I'd rather you would stop it with a kiss.

Miss. A kiss! marry come up, my dirty cousin; are you no sicker? Lord! I wonder what fool it was that first invented kissing!

Neverout. Well, I'm very dry.

Miss. Then you're the better to burn, and the worse to fry.

Lady

Lady Anſw. God bleſs you colonel; you have a good ſtroke with you.

Col. O madam; formerly I could eat all, but now I leave nothing; I eat but one meal a day.

Miſs. What! I ſuppoſe, colonel, that is from morning till night.

Neverout. Faith, miſs; and well was his wont.

Ld. Smart. Pray, lady *Anſwerall,* taſte this bit of veniſon.

Lady Anſw. I hope, your lordſhip will ſet me a good example.

Ld. Smart. Here's a glaſs of cyder fill'd: miſs, you muſt drink it.

Miſs. Indeed, my lord, I can't.

Neverout. Come miſs; better belly burſt, than good liquor be loſt.

Miſs. Piſh! well in life there was never any thing ſo teizing; I had rather ſhed it in my ſhoes: I wiſh it were in your guts, for my ſhare.

Ld. Smart. Mr. *Neverout,* you han't taſted my cyder yet.

Neverout. No, my lord; I have been juſt eating ſoupe; and they ſay, if one drinks

drinks with one's porridge, one will cough in one's grave.

Ld. Smart. Come, take miſs's glaſs, ſhe wiſh'd it was in your guts; let her have her wiſh for once: ladies can't abide to have their inclinations croſs'd.

Lady Smart. [*to Sir John*] I think, ſir *John*, you have not taſted the veniſon yet.

Sir John. I ſeldom eat it, madam; however, pleaſe to ſend me a little of the cruſt.

Ld. Sparkiſh. Why, ſir *John*, you had as good eat the devil, as the broth he is boil'd in.

Col. Well, this eating and drinking takes away a body's ſtomach, as lady *Anſwerall* ſays.

Neverout. I have dined as well as my lord-mayor.

Miſs. I thought I could have eaten this wing of a chicken; but my eye's bigger than my belly.

Ld. Smart. Indeed, lady *Anſwerall*, you have eaten nothing.

Lady Anſw. Pray, my lord, ſee all the

the bones on my plate: they fay, a carpenter's known by his chips.

Neverout. Mifs, will you reach me that glafs of jelly?

Mifs. [*giving it to him*] You fee, 'tis but afk and have.

Neverout. Mifs, I would have a bigger glafs.

Mifs. What? you don't know your own mind; you are neither well, full nor fafting; I think that is enough.

Neverout. Ay, one of the enoughs; I am fure it is little enough.

Mifs. Yes; but you know, fweet things are bad for the teeth.

Neverout. [*to Lady Anfw.*] Madam, I don't like that part of the veal you fent me.

Lady Anfw. Well, Mr. *Neverout*, I find you are a true *Englifhman*, you never know when you are well.

Col. Well, I have made my whole dinner of beef.

Lady Anfw. Why, colonel, a belly-full's a belly-full, if it be but of wheat-ftraw.

Col. Well, after all, kitchen phyfic is the beft phyfic.

Ld.

DIALOGUE II.

Lady Smart. And the best doctors in the world are doctor *Dyet*, doctor *Quiet*, and doctor *Merryman*.

Ld. Sparkish. What do you think of a little house well fill'd?

Sir John. And a little land well till'd?

Col. Ay; and a little wife well will'd?

Neverout. My lady *Smart*, pray help me to some of the breast of that goose.

Ld. Smart. Tom, I have heard that goose upon goose is false heraldry.

Miss. What! will you never have done stuffing?

Ld. Smart. This goose is quite raw: well, God sends meat, but the devil sends cooks.

Neverout. Miss, can you tell which is the gander, the white goose or the grey goose.

Miss. They say, a fool will ask more questions than the wisest body can answer.

Col. Indeed, miss, *Tom Neverout* has posed you.

Miss. Why, colonel, every dog has his day; but I believe I shall never see a goose again without thinking on Mr. *Neverout.*

Ld. Smart. Well said, miss; faith, girl, thou hast brought thyself off cleverly. *Tom,* what say you that?

Col. Faith, *Tom* is nonplust; he looks plaguily down in the mouth.

Miss. Why, my lord, you see he is the provokingest creature in life; I believe there is not such another in the varsal world.

Lady Answ. Oh, miss! the world's a wide place.

Neverout. Well, miss, I'll give you leave to call me any thing, if you don't call me spade.

Ld. Smart. Well, but after all, *Tom,* can you tell me what's *Latin* for a goose?

Neverout. O my lord, I know that; why *brandy* is *Latin* for a goose, and *face* is *Latin* for a candle.

Miss. Is that manners, to shew your learning before ladies? Methinks you are gown very brisk of a sudden; I think the man's glad he's alive.

Sir John. The devil take your wit, if this be wit; for it spoils company: pray, Mr.

DIALOGUE II.

Mr. *Butler*, bring me a dram after my goose; 'tis very good for the wholesomes.

Ld. Smart. Come, bring me the loaf; I sometimes love to cut my own bread.

Miss. I suppose, my lord, you lay longest a-bed to-day.

Ld. Smart. Miss, if I had said so, I should have told a fib; I warrant you lay a-bed till the cows came home: but, miss, shall I cut you a little crust now my hand is in?

Miss. If you please, my lord, a bit of under-crust.

Neverout. [*whispering Miss*] I find you love to lie under.

Miss. [*aloud, pushing him from her*] What does the man mean! Sir, I don't understand you at all *.

Neverout. Come, all quarrels laid aside: here, miss, may you live a thousand years.
[*He drinks to her.*
Miss. Pray, sir, don't stint me.

* Miss discovers her understanding by the manner in which she denies it, an inconsistency so common that it deserves a note. See p. 186.

Ld. Smart. Sir *John,* will you taste my *October?* I think it is very good; but I believe not equal to yours in *Darbyshire.*

Sir John. My lord, I beg your pardon; but they say, the devil made askers.

Ld. Smart. [*to the butler*] Here, bring up the great tankard full of *October* for sir *John.*

Col. [*drinking to Miss*] Miss, your health; may you live all the days of your life.

Lady Answ. Well, miss, you'll certainly be soon married; here's two batchelors drinking to you at once.

Lady Smart. Indeed, miss, I believe you were wrapt in your mother's smock, you are so well belov'd.

Miss. Where's my knife? sure I han't eaten it: Oh, here it is.

Sir John. No, miss; but your maidenhead hangs in your light.

Miss. Pray, sir *John,* is that a *Darbyshire* compliment? Here, Mr. *Neverout,* will you take this piece of rabbit that you bid me carve for you?

Neverout. I don't know.

Miss. Why, take it, or let it alone.

Neverout. I will.

Miss. What will you?

Neverout. Why, I'll take it, or let it alone.

Miss. You are a provoking creature.

Sir John [*talking with a glass of wine in his hand*] I remember a farmer in our country ---

Ld. Smart. [*interrupting him*] Pray, sir *John*, did you ever hear of parson *Palmer*?

Sir John. No, my lord; what of him?

Ld. Smart. Why, he used to preach over his liquor.

Sir John. I beg your lordship's pardon; here's your lordship's health: I'd drink it up, if it were a mile to the bottom.

Lady Smart. Mr. *Neverout*, have you been at the new play?

Neverout. Yes, madam, I went the first night.

Lady Smart. Well, and how did it take?

Neverout. Why, madam, the poet is damn'd.

Sir John. God forgive you! that's very uncharitable: you ought not to judge so rashly of any christian.

Neverout [*whispers Lady Smart*] Was ever such a dunce? How well he knows the town! See how he stares like a stuck-pig! Well, but, sir *John*, are you acquainted with any of our fine ladies yet?

Sir John. No; damn your fire-ships, I have a wife of my own.

Lady Smart. Pray, my lady *Answerall*, how do you like these preserv'd oranges?

Lady Answ. Indeed, madam, the only fault I find is, that they are too good.

Lady Smart. O madam; I have heard 'em say, that too good is stark naught.

Miss *drinking part of a glass of wine.*

Neverout. Pray, let me drink your snuff.

Miss. No, indeed, you shan't drink after me; for you'll know my thoughts.

Neverout. I know them already; you are thinking of a good husband. Besides, I can tell your meaning by your mumping.

Lady

DIALOGUE II.

Lady Smart. Pray, my lord, did not you order the butler to bring up a tankard of our *October* to fir *John?* I believe, they stay to brew it.

The Butler *brings up the tankard to sir* John.

Sir John. Won't your ladyship please to drink first.

Lady Smart. No, sir *John*; 'tis in a very good hand; I'll pledge you.

Col. [*to Ld. Smart.*] My lord, I love *October* as well as sir *John*; and I hope, you won't make fish of one, and flesh of another.

Ld. Smart. Colonel, you're heartily welcome. Come, sir *John*, take it by word of mouth, and then give it the colonel.

Sir John *drinks.*

Ld. Smart. Well, sir *John*, how do you like it?

Sir John. Not as well as my own in *Darbyshire*; 'tis plaguy small.

Lady Smart. I never taste malt liquor; but they say 'tis well hopt.

Sir John. Hopt! why, if it had hopp'd a little further, it would have hopp'd into the river. O my lord, my ale is meat, drink, and cloth; it will make a cat speak, and a wife man dumb.

Lady Smart. I was told, ours was very strong.

Sir John. Ay, madam, strong of the water; I believe the brewer forgot the malt, or the river was too near him. Faith, it is mere whip-belly-vengeance; he that drinks most has the worst share.

Col. I believe, sir *John*, ale is as plenty as water at your house.

Sir John. Why, faith, at *Christmas* we have many comers and goers; and they must not be sent away without a cup of *Christmas* ale, for fear they should p--s behind the door.

Lady Smart. I hear, sir *John* has the nicest garden in *England*; they say, 'tis kept so clean, that you can't find a place where to spit.

Sir John. O madam; you are pleased to say so.

Lady Smart. But, sir *John*, your ale is terrible strong and heady in *Derbyshire*,

and

DIALOGUE II.

and will foon make one drunk and fick; what do you then?

Sir John. Why, indeed, it is apt to fox one; but our way is, to take a hare of the fame dog next morning. I take a new-laid egg for breakfaft; and faith, one fhould drink as much after an egg as after an ox.

Ld. Smart. Tom *Neverout,* will you tafte a glafs of *October?*

Neverout. No, faith, my lord; I like your wine, and I won't put a churl upon a gentleman; your honour's claret is good enough for me.

Lady Smart. What! is this pigeon left for manners? colonel, fhall I fend you the legs and rump?

Col. Madam, I could not eat a bit more, if the houfe was full.

Ld. Smart. [*carving a partridge*] Well; one may ride to *Rumford* upon this knife, it is fo blunt.

Lady Anfw. My lord, I beg your pardon; but they fay, an ill workman never had good tools.

Ld. Smart. Will your lordfhip have a wing of it?

Ld.

Ld. Sparkish. No, my lord; I love the wing of an ox a great deal better.

Ld. Smart. I'm always cold after eating.

Col. My lord, they say, that's a sign of long life.

Ld. Smart. Ay; I believe I shall live till all my friends are weary of me.

Col. Pray, does any body here hate cheese? I would be glad of a bit.

Ld. Smart. An odd kind of fellow dined with me t'other day; and when the cheese came upon the table, he pretended to faint; so somebody said, Pray take away the cheese: No, said I; pray, take away the fool: said I well?

Here a loud and large laugh.

Col. Faith, my lord, you serv'd the coxcomb right enough; and therefore I wish we had a bit of your lordship's *Oxfordshire* cheese.

Ld. Smart. Come, hang saving; bring us up a halfp'orth of cheese

Lady Answ. They say, cheese digests every thing but itself.

DIALOGUE II.

A Footman brings a great whole cheese.

Ld. Sparkish. Ay; this would look handsome, if any body should come in.

Sir John. Well; I'm weily broften, as they sayn in *Lancashire*.

Lady Smart. O! sir *John*; I wou'd I had something to broft you withal.

Ld. Smart. Come, they say, 'tis merry in the hall when beards wag all.

Lady Smart. Miss, shall I help you to some cheese, or will you carve for yourself?

Neverout. I'll hold fifty pounds, miss won't cut the cheese.

Miss. Pray, why so, Mr. *Neverout?*

Neverout. Oh, there is a reason, and you know it well enough.

Miss. I can't for my life understand what the gentleman means.

Ld. Smart. Pray, *Tom*, change the discourse: in troth you are too bad.

Col. [*whispers Neverout*] Smoke miss; faith you have made her fret like gum taffety.

Lady Smart. Well, but, miss, (hold your

your tongue, Mr. *Neverout)* shall I cut you a piece of cheese?

Miss. No, really, madam; I have dined this half hour.

Lady Smart. What! quick at meat, quick at work, they say.

Sir John *nods.*

Ld. Smart. What! are you sleep, sir *John?* do you sleep after dinner?

Sir John. Yes faith; I sometimes take a nap after my * pipe; for when the belly is full, the bones would be at rest.

Lady Smart. Come, colonel; help yourself, and your friends will love you the better. [*to Lady Answ.*] madam your ladyship eats nothing.

Lady Answ. Lord, madam, I have fed

---

* It may be observed in this passage, and many others, that the author gave himself no trouble to render the drama of this piece perfect. Sir *John* is here supposed to have *smoked*, and the lady is immediately afterwards pressed *to eat.* His principal view was to string all the phrases that are uttered by rote one upon another, without the assistance of any other language to introduce or correct them, the drama therefore must be regarded merely as a vehicle; and whoever considers the difficulty of that which is effected, will scarce be so unreasonable as to censure the writer for not effecting more.

DIALOGUE II.

like a farmer; I shall grow as fat as a porpoise; I swear, my jaws are weary of chewing.

Col. I have a mind to eat a piece of that sturgeon, but fear it will make me sick.

Neverout. A rare soldier indeed! let it alone, and I warrant it won't hurt you.

Col. Well; it wou'd vex a dog to see a pudden creep.

Sir John *rises.*

Ld. Smart. Sir *John,* what are you doing?

Sir John. Swolks, I must be going, by'r lady; I have earnest business; I must do as the beggars do, go away when I have got enough.

Ld. Smart. Well; but stay till this bottle's out; you know, the man was hang'd that left his liquor behind him: and besides, a cup in the pate is a mile in the gate; and a spur in the head is worth two in the heel.

Sir John. Come then; one brimmer to all your healths. [*The footman gives him*

him a glafs half full] Pray, friend, what was the reft of this glafs made for? an inch at the top, friend, is worth two at the bottom. *He gets a brimmer, and drinks it off*] Well, there's no deceit in a brimmer, and there's no falfe *Latin* in this; your wine is excellent good, fo I thank you for the next, for I am fure of this: madam, has your ladyfhip any commands in *Darbyfhire?* I muft go fifteen miles to-night.

Lady Smart. None, fir *John*, but to take care of yourfelf; and my moft humble fervice to your lady unknown.

Sir John. Well, madam, I can but love and thank you.

Lady Smart. Here, bring water to wafh; tho' really, you have all eaten fo little, that you have not need to wafh your mouths.

Ld. Smart. But, prithee, fir *John* ftay a while longer.

Sir John. No, my lord; I am to fmoke a pipe with a friend before I leave the town.

Col. Why, fir *John*, had not you better fet out to-morrow?

DIALOGUE II.

Sir John. Colonel, you forget to-morrow is *Sunday.*

Col. Now I always love to begin a journey on *Sundays,* becaufe I fhall have the prayers of the church, to preferve all that travel by land, or by water.

Sir John. Well, colonel; thou art a mad fellow to make a prieft of.

Neverout. Fie, fir *John,* do you take tobacco? How can you make a chimney of your mouth?

Sir John. [*to Neverout*] What! you don't fmoke, I warrant you, but you fmock. (Ladies, I beg your pardon.) Colonel, do you never fmoke?

Col. No, fir *John;* but I take a pipe fometimes.

Sir John. I'faith, one of your finical *London* blades dined with me laft year in *Darbyfhire;* fo, after dinner, I took a pipe; fo my gentleman turn'd away his head: fo, faid I, what, fir, do you never fmoke? fo, he anfwered as you do, colonel; no, but I fometimes take a pipe: fo he took a pipe in his hand, and fiddled with it till he broke it: fo, faid I, pray,

pray, fir, can you make a pipe? fo, he said no; fo, faid I, why then, fir, if you can't make pipe, you fhould not break a pipe; fo, we all laugh'd.

Ld. Smart. Well; bnt, fir *John*, they fay, that the corruption of pipes is the generation of ftoppers.

Sir John. Colonel, I hear you go fometimes to *Darbyfhire*; I wifh you would come and foul a plate with me.

Col. I hope, you will give me a foldier's bottle.

Sir John. Come, and try. Mr. *Neverout*, you are a town-wit; can you tell me what kind of herb is tobacco?

Neverout. Why, an *Indian* herb, fir *John*.

Sir John. No, 'tis a pot-herb; and fo here's t'ye in a pot of my lord's *October*.

Lady Smart. I hear, fir *John*, fince you are married, you have forfwore the town.

Sir John. No, madam; I never forfwore any thing but the building of churches.

Lady

DIALOGUE II.

Lady Smart. Well; but sir *John*, when may we hope to see you again in *London*?

Sir John. Why, madam, not till the ducks have eat up the dirt, as the children say.

Neverout. Come, sir *John:* I foresee it will rain terribly.

Lady Smart. Come, sir *John*, do nothing rashly; let us drink first.

Ld. Sparkish. I know sir *John* will go, tho' he was sure it would rain cats and dogs: but pray, stay, sir *John*; you'll be time enough to go to bed by candle-light.

Ld. Smart. Why, sir *John*, if you must needs go; while you stay, make use of your time: here's my service to you, a health to our friends in *Darby-shire:* come, sit down; let us put off the evil hour as long as we can.

Sir John. Faith, I could not drink a drop more, if the house was full.

Col. Why, sir *John*, you used to love a glass of good wine in former times.

Sir John. Why, so I do still, colonel; but

but a man may love his houfe very well, without riding on the ridge: befides, I muft be with my wife on *Tuefday*, or there will be the devil and all to pay.

Col. Well, if you go to-day, I wifh you may be wet to the fkin.

Sir John. Ay; but they fay, the prayers of the wicked won't prevail.

Sir John *takes leave, and goes away.*

Ld. Smart. Well, mifs, how do you like fir *John?*

Mifs. Why, I think, he's a little upon the filly, or fo: I believe, he has not all the wit in the world: but I don't pretend to be a judge.

Neverout. Faith, I believe, he was bred at *Hog's Norton*, where the pigs play upon the organs.

Ld. Sparkifh. Why, *Tom*, I thought you and he were hand and glove.

Neverout. Faith, he fhall have a clean threfhold for me; I never darkened his door in my life, neither in town nor country; but he's a queer old duke, by my confcience; and yet, after all, I take him to be more knave than fool.

Lady

Lady Smart. Well, come; a man's a man, if he has but a nose on his face.

Col. I was once with him and some other company over a bottle; and, egad, he fell asleep, and snor'd so hard, that we thought he was driving his hogs to market.

Neverout. Why, what! you can have no more of a cat than her skin; you can't make a silk purse out of a sow's ear.

Ld. Sparkish. Well, since he's gone, the devil go with him and sixpence; and there's money and company too.

Neverout. Faith, he's a true country put. Pray, miss, let me ask you a question?

Miss. Well; but don't ask questions with a dirty face: I warrant, what you have to say will keep cold.

Col. Come, my lord, against you are disposed; here's to all that love and honour you.

Ld. Sparkish. Ay, that was always *Dick Nimble*'s health. I'm sure you know he's dead.

Col. Dead! well, my lord, you love to be a messenger of ill news: I'm heartily sorry; but, my lord, we must all die.

Neverout. I knew him very well: but, pray, how came he to die?

Miss. There's a question! you talk like a poticary: why, because he could live no longer.

Neverout. Well; rest his soul: we must live by the living, and not by the dead.

Ld. Sparkish. You know, his house was burnt down to the ground.

Col. Yes; it was in the news. Why fire and water are good servants, but they are very bad masters.

Ld. Smart. Here, take away, and set down a bottle of *Burgundy*. Ladies, you'll stay and drink a glass of wine before you go to your tea.

All taken away, and the wine set down, etc.

Miss *gives* Neverout *a smart pinch.*

Neverout. Lord, miss, what d'ye mean? d'ye think I have no feeling?

Miss. I'm forc'd to pinch, for the times are hard.

Neverout. [*giving Miss a pinch.*] Take that,

that, miſs; what's ſauce for a gooſe is ſauce for a gander.

Miſs. [*ſcreaming*] Well, Mr. *Neverout*, that ſhall neither go to heaven nor hell with you.

Neverout. [*takes Miſs by the hand*] Come, miſs, let us lay all quarrels aſide, and be friends.

Miſs. Don't be ſo teizing : you plague a body ſo! can't you keep your filthy hands to yourſelf?

Neverout. Pray, miſs, where did you get that pick-tooth caſe?

Miſs. I came honeſtly by it.

Neverout. I'm ſure it was mine, for I loſt juſt ſuch a one; nay, I don't tell you a lye.

Miſs. No; if you lye, it is much.

Neverout. Well; I'm ſure 'tis mine.

Miſs. What! you think every thing is yours, but a little the king has.

Neverout. Colonel, you have ſeen my fine pick-tooth caſe; don't you think this is the very ſame?

Col. Indeed, miſs, it is very like it.

Miſs. Ay; what he ſays, you'll ſwear.

Neverout. Well; but I'll prove it to be mine. *Miſs.*

Miss. Ay; do if you can.

Neverout. Why, what's yours is mine, and what's mine is my own.

Miss. Well, run on till you're weary; nobody holds you.

Neverout *gapes.*

Col. What, Mr. *Neverout,* do you gape for preferment?

Neverout. Faith, I may gape long enough, before it falls into my mouth.

Lady Smart. Mr. *Neverout,* my lord and I intend to beat up your quarters one of these days: I hear, you live high.

Neverout. Yes, faith, madam; I live high, and lodge in a garret.

Col. But, miss, I forgot to tell you, that Mr. *Neverout* got the devilisheft fall in the park to-day.

Miss. I hope he did not hurt the ground: but how was it, Mr. *Neverout?* I wish I had been there to laugh.

Neverout. Why, madam, it was a place where a cuckold had been buried, and one of his horns sticking out, I happened to stumble against it; that was all.

DIALOGUE II.

Lady Smart. Ladies, let us leave the gentlemen to themselves; I think it is time to go to our tea.

Lady Anſw. and *Miſs.* My lords and gentlemen, your moſt humble ſervant.

Ld. Smart. Well, ladies, we'll wait on you an hour hence.

The gentlemen alone.

Ld. Smart. Come, *John*, bring us a freſh bottle.

Col. Ay, my lord; and pray, let him carry off the dead men, as we ſay in the army. [*Meaning the empty bottles.*

Ld. Sparkiſh. Mr. *Neverout*, pray, is not that bottle full?

Neverout. Yes, my lord; full of emptineſs.

Ld. Smart. And, d'ye hear, *John*, bring clean glaſſes.

Col. I'll keep mine; for I think, the wine is the beſt liquor to waſh glaſſes in.

DIALOGUE III.

The ladies at their tea.

Lady Smart.

WELL, ladies; now let us have a cup of discourse to ourselves.

Lady Answ. What do you think of your friend, sir *John Spendall?*

Lady Smart. Why, madam, 'tis happy for him, that his father was born before him.

Miss. They say, he makes a very ill husband to my lady.

Lady Answ. But he must be allow'd to be the fondest father in the world.

Lady Smart. Ay, madam, that's true; for they say, the devil is kind to his own.

Miss. I am told, my lady manages him to admiration.

Lady Smart. That I believe, for she's as cunning as a dead pig, but not half so honest.

Lady Answ. They say, she's quite a stranger to all his gallantries.

DIALOGUE III.

Lady Smart. Not at all; but you know, there's none so blind as they that won't see.

Miss. O madam, I am told, she watches him as a cat would watch a mouse.

Lady Answ. Well, if she ben't foully belied, she pays him in his own coin.

Lady Smart. Madam, I fancy I know your thoughts, as well as if I were within you.

Lady Answ. Madam, I was t'other day in company with Mrs. *Clatter*; I find she gives herself airs of being acquainted with your ladyship.

Miss. Oh, the hideous creature! did you observe her nails? they were long enough to scratch her grannum out of her grave.

Lady Smart. Well, she and *Tom Gosling* were banging compliments backwards and forwards: it look'd like two asses scrubbing one another.

Miss. Ay, claw me, and I'll claw you: but, pray, madam, who were the company?

Lady Smart. Why there was all the world, and his wife; there was Mrs. *Clatter,*

Clatter, lady *Singular*, the countefs of *Talkham*, (I fhould have named her firft) *Tom Gofling*, and fome others, whom I have forgot.

Lady Anfw. I think the countefs is very fickly.

Lady Smart. Yes, madam; fhe'll never fcratch a grey head, I promife her.

Mifs. And, pray, what was your converfation?

Lady Smart. Why, Mrs. *Clatter* had all the talk to herfelf, and was perpetually complaining of her misfortunes.

Lady Anfw. She brought her hufband ten thoufand pounds; fhe has a town houfe and country-houfe: would the woman have her a--- hung with points?

Lady Smart. She would fain be at the top of the houfe before the ftairs are built.

Mifs. Well, comparifons are odious; but fhe's as like her hufband as if fhe were fpit out of his mouth; as like as one egg is to another: pray, how was fhe dreft?

Lady Smart. Why, fhe was as fine as fi'pence; but, truly, I thought there was more coft than worfhip.

Lady

Lady Answ. I don't know her husband: pray, what is he?

Lady Smart. Why, he's a councellor of the law; you must know he came to us as drunk as *David*'s sow.

Miss. What kind of creature is he?

Lady Smart. You must know, the man and his wife are coupled like rabbets, a fat and a lean; he's as fat as a porpus, and she's one of *Pharaoh*'s lean kine: the ladies and *Tom Gosling* were proposing a party at quadrille; but he refus'd to make one: Damn your cards, said he, they are the devil's books.

Lady Answ. A dull, unmannerly brute! well, God send him more wit, and me more money.

Miss. Lord! madam, I would not keep such company for the world.

Lady Smart. O miss, 'tis nothing when you are used to it: besides, you know, for want of company, welcome trumpery.

Miss. Did your ladyship play?

Lady Smart. Yes, and won; so I came off with fidler's fare, meat, drink, and money.

Lady Answ. Ay; what says *Pluck?*

Miss. Well, my elbow itches; I shall change bedfellows.

Lady Smart. And my right hand itches; I shall receive money.

Lady Answ. And my right eye itches; I shall cry.

Lady Smart. Miss, I hear your friend mistress *Giddy* has discarded *Dick Shuttle:* pray, has she got another lover?

Miss. I hear of none.

Lady Smart. Why, the fellow's rich; and I think she was a fool to throw out her dirty water before she got clean.

Lady Answ. Miss, that's a very handsome gown of yours, and finely made; very genteel.

Miss. I am glad your ladyship likes it.

Lady Answ. Your lover will be in raptures; it becomes you admirably.

Miss; Ay; I assure you I won't take it as I have done; if this won't fetch him, the devil fetch him, say I.

Lady Smart. [*to Lady Answ.*] Pray, madam, when did you see sir *Peter Muckworm?*

DIALOGUE III.

Lady Anfw. Not this fortnight; I hear he's laid up with the gout.

Lady Smart. What does he do for it?

Lady Anfw. I hear he's weary of doctoring it, and now makes ufe of nothing but patience and flannel.

Mifs. Pray, how does he and my lady agree?

Lady Anfw. You know he loves her as the devil loves holy water.

Mifs. They fay, fhe plays deep with fharpers, that cheat her of her money.

Lady Anfw. Upon my word they muft rife early that would cheat her of her money; fharp's the word with her; diamonds cut diamonds.

Mifs. Well, but I was affur'd from a good hand, that fhe loft at one fitting to the tune of a hundred guineas; make money of that.

Lady Smart. Well, but do you hear that Mrs. *Plump* is brought to bed at laft?

Mifs. And pray, what has God fent her?

Lady Smart. Why, guefs if you can.

Mifs. A boy I fuppofe.

Lady Smart. No, you are out; guess again.

Miss. A girl then.

Lady Smart. You have hit it; I believe you are a witch.

Miss. O madam, the gentlemen say, all fine ladies are witches; but I pretend to no such thing.

Lady Answ. Well, she had good luck to draw *Tom Plump* into wedlock; she ris' with her a--- upwards.

Miss. Fie, madam; what do you mean?

Lady Smart. O miss, 'tis nothing what we say among ourselves.

Miss. Ay, madam; but they say, hedges have eyes, and walls have ears.

Lady Answ. Well, miss, I can't help it; you know, I'm old Tell-truth; I love to call a spade a spade.

Lady Smart. [*mistakes the tea-tongs for the spoon*] What! I think my wits are a wool-gathering to-day.

Miss. Why, madam, there was but a right and a wrong.

Lady Smart. Miss, I hear that you and lady *Coupler* are as great as cup and can.

DIALOGUE III.

Lady Anſw. Ay, miſs, as great as the devil and the earl of *Kent*.

Lady Smart. Nay, I am told you meet together with as much love as there is between the old cow and the hay-ſtack.

Miſs. I own I love her very well; but there's difference betwixt ſtaring and ſtark mad.

Lady Smart. They ſay, ſhe begins to grow fat.

Miſs. Fat! ay, fat as a hen in the forehead.

Lady Smart. Indeed, lady *Anſwerall*, (pray forgive me) I think your ladyſhip looks thinner than when I ſaw you laſt.

Miſs. Indeed, madam, I think not; but your ladyſhip is one of *Job*'s comforters.

Lady Anſw. Well, no matter how I look; I am bought and ſold: but really, miſs, you are ſo very obliging, that I wiſh I were a handſome young lord for your ſake.

Miſs. O madam, your love's a million.

Lady Smart. [*to Lady Anſw.*] Madam, will your ladyſhip let me wait on you to the play to-morrow?

Lady Anſw. Madam, it becomes me to wait on your ladyſhip.

Miſs. What, then, I'm turn'd out for a wrangler.

The gentlemen come in to the ladies to drink tea.

Miſs. Mr. *Neverout*, we wanted you ſadly; you are always out of the way when you ſhould be hang'd.

Neverout. You wanted me! pray, miſs, how do you look when you lie?

Miſs. Better than you when you cry. Manners indeed! I find you mend like ſour ale in ſummer.

Neverout. I beg your pardon, miſs; I only meant, when you lie alone.

Miſs. That's well turn'd; one turn more would have turn'd you down ſtairs.

Neverout. Come, miſs, be kind for once, and order me a diſh of coffee.

Miſs. Pray, go yourſelf; let us wear out the oldeſt: beſides, I can't go, for I have a bone in my leg.

Col They ſay, a woman need but look on her apron-ſtring to find an excuſe.

DIALOGUE III.

Neverout. Why, miss, you are grown so peevish, a dog would not live with you.

Miss. Mr. *Neverout*, I beg your diversion; no offence, I hope; but truly in a little time you intend to make the colonel as bad as yourself; and that's as bad as can be.

Neverout. My lord, don't you think miss improves wonderfully of late? why, miss, if I spoil the colonel, I hope you will use him as you do me; for you know, love me, love my dog.

Col. How's that, *Tom?* Say that again: why, if I am a dog, shake hands, brother.

Here a great, loud, long laugh.

Ld. Smart. But pray, gentlemen, why always so severe upon poor miss? on my conscience, colonel and *Tom Neverout*, one of you two are both knaves.

Col. My lady *Answerall*, I intend to do myself the honour of dining with your ladyship to-morrow.

Lady Answ. Ay, colonel, do if you can.

Miss. I'm sure you'll be glad to be welcome.

Col. Miss, I thank you; and to reward you

you, I'll come and drink tea with you in the morning.

Miss. Colonel, there's two words to that bargain.

Col. [*to Lady Smart.*] Your ladyship has a very fine watch; well may you wear it.

Lady Smart. It is none of mine, colonel.

Col. Pray, whose is it then?

Lady Smart. Why, 'tis my lord's; for they say, a marry'd woman has nothing of her own, but her wedding-ring and her hair-lace: but if women had been the law-makers, it would have been better.

Col. This watch seems to be quite new.

Lady Smart. No, sir; it has been twenty years in my lord's family; but *Quare* put a new case and dial-plate to it.

Neverout. Why, that's for all the world like the man, who swore he kept the same knife forty years, only he sometimes changed the haft, and sometimes the blade.

Ld. Smart. Well, *Tom*, to give the devil his due, thou art a right woman's man.

Col. Odd-so! I have broke the hinge of

DIALOGUE III.

of my snuff-box; I'm undone besides the loss.

Miss. Alack-a-day, colonel! I vow I had rather have found forty shillings.

Neverout. Why, colonel; all that I can say to comfort you, is, that you must mend it with a new one.

Miss *laughs.*

Col. What, miss! you can't laugh, but you must shew your teeth.

Miss. I'm sure you shew your teeth, when you can't bite: well, thus it must be, if we sell ale.

Neverout. Miss, you smell very sweet; I hope you don't carry perfumes.

Miss. Perfumes! No, sir; I'd have you to know, it is nothing but the grain of my skin.

Col. Tom, you have a good nose to make a poor man's sow.

Ld. Sparkish. So, ladies and gentlemen, methinks you are very witty upon one another: come, box it about; 'twill come to my father at last.

Col. Why, my lord, you see miss has no mercy; I wish she were marry'd; but I

doubt

doubt the grey mare would prove the better horse.

Miss. Well, God forgive you for that wish.

Ld. Sparkish. Never fear him, miss.

Miss. What, my lord, do you think I was born in a wood, to be afraid of an owl?

Ld. Smart. What have you to say to that, colonel?

Neverout. O my lord, my friend the colonel scorns to set his wit against a child.

Miss. Scornful dogs will eat dirty puddings.

Col. Well, miss; they say, a woman's tongue is the last thing about her that dies; therefore let's kiss and friends.

Miss. Hands off! that's meat for your master.

Ld. Sparkish. Faith, colonel, you are for ale and cakes: but after all, miss, you are too severe; you would not meddle with your match.

Miss. All they can say goes in at one ear and out at t'other for me, I can assure you: only I wish they would be quiet, and let me drink my tea.

Neverout. What! I warrant you think all is lost that goes beside your own mouth.

Miss. Pray, Mr. *Neverout*, hold your tongue for once, if it be possible; one would think you were a woman in man's cloaths, by your prating.

Neverout. No, miss; it is not handsome to see one hold one's tongue: besides, I should slobber my fingers.

Col. Miss, did you never hear, that three women and a goose are enough to make a market?

Miss. I'm sure, if Mr. *Neverout* or you were among them, it would make a fair.

Footman *comes in.*

Lady Smart. Here, take away the tea-table, and bring up candles.

Lady Answ. O madam, no candles yet, I beseech you; don't let us burn day-light.

Neverout. I dare swear, miss for her part will never burn day-light, if she can help it.

Miss. Lord, Mr. *Neverout*, one can't hear one's own ears for you.

Lady Smart. Indeed, madam, it is blind man's holiday; we shall soon be all of a colour.

Neverout. Why, then, miss, we may kiss where we like best.

Miss. Fogh! these men talk of nothing but kissing. [*She spits.*

Neverout. What, miss, does it make your mouth water?

Lady Smart. It is as good be in the dark as without light; therefore pray bring in candles: they say, women and linnen shew best by candle-light: come, gentlemen, are you for a party at quadrille?

Col. I'll make one with you three ladies.

Lady Answ. I'll sit down, and be a stander-by.

Lady Smart [*to Lady Answ.*] Madam, does your ladyship never play?

Col. Yes; I suppose her ladyship plays sometimes for an egg at *Easter.*

Neverout. Ay; and a kiss at *Christmas.*

Lady Answ. Come, Mr. *Neverout*, hold your tongue, and mind your knitting.

Neverout. With all my heart; kiſs my wife, and welcome.

The Colonel, *Mr.* Neverout, *Lady* Smart *and* Miſs *go to quadrille, and ſit there till three in the morning.*

They riſe from cards.

Lady Smart. Well, miſs, you'll have a ſad huſband, you have ſuch good luck at cards.

Neverout. Indeed, miſs, you dealt me ſad cards; if you deal ſo ill by your friends, what will you do with your enemies?

Lady Anſw. I'm ſure 'tis time for honeſt folks to be a-bed.

Miſs. Indeed my eyes draw ſtraws.

She's almoſt aſleep.

Neverout. Why, miſs, if you fall aſleep, ſomebody may get a pair of gloves.

Col. I'm going to the Land of *Nod.*

Neverout. Faith, I'm for *Bedfordſhire.*

Lady Smart. I'm ſure I ſhall ſleep without rocking.

Neverout. Miſs, I hope you'll dream of your ſweetheart.

Miss. Oh, no doubt of it: I believe I shan't be able to sleep for dreaming of him.

Col. [*to Miss.*] Madam, shall I have the honour to escort you?

Miss. No, colonel, I thank you; my mamma has sent her chair and footmen. Well, my lady *Smart*, I'll give you revenge whenever you please.

Footman *comes in.*

Footman. Madam, the chairs are waiting.

They all take their chairs, and go off.

ALSO AVAILABLE FROM THOEMMES PRESS

For Her Own Good – A Series of Conduct Books

Cœlebs in Search of a Wife
Hannah More
With a new introduction by Mary Waldron
ISBN 1 85506 383 2 : 288pp : 1808–9 edition : £14.75

Female Replies to Swetnam the Woman-Hater
Various
With a new introduction by Charles Butler
ISBN 1 85506 379 4 : 336pp : 1615–20 edition : £15.75

A Complete Collection of Genteel and Ingenious Conversation
Jonathan Swift
With a new introduction by the Rt Hon. Michael Foot
ISBN 1 85506 380 8 : 224pp : 1755 edition : £13.75

Thoughts on the Education of Daughters
Mary Wollstonecraft
With a new introduction by Janet Todd
ISBN 1 85506 381 6 : 192pp : 1787 edition : £13.75

The Young Lady's Pocket Library, or Parental Monitor
Various
With a new introduction by Vivien Jones
ISBN 1 85506 382 4 : 352pp : 1790 edition : £15.75

Also available as a 5 volume set : ISBN 1 85506 378 6
Special Set Price: £65.00

Her Write His Name

Old Kensington *and* The Story of Elizabeth
Anne Isabella Thackeray
With a new introduction by Esther Schwartz-McKinzie
ISBN 1 85506 388 3 : 496pp : 1873 & 1876 editions : £17.75

Shells from the Sands of Time
Rosina Bulwer Lytton
With a new introduction by Marie Mulvey Roberts
ISBN 1 85506 386 7 : 272pp : 1876 edition : £14.75

Platonics
Ethel Arnold
With a new introduction by Phyllis Wachter
ISBN 1 85506 389 1 : 160pp : 1894 edition : £13.75

The Continental Journals 1798-1820
Dorothy Wordsworth
With a new introduction by Helen Boden
ISBN 1 85506 385 9 : 472pp : New edition : £17.75

Her Life in Letters
Alice James
Edited with a new introduction by Linda Anderson
ISBN 1 85506 387 5 : 320pp : New : £15.75

Also available as a 5 volume set : ISBN 1 8556 384 0
Special set price : £70.00

Subversive Women

The Art of Ingeniously Tormenting
Jane Collier
With a new introduction by Judith Hawley
ISBN 1 8556 246 1 : 292pp : 1757 edition : £14.75

Appeal of One Half the Human Race, Women, Against the Pretensions of the Other Half, Men, to Retain them in Political, and thence in Civil and Domestic, Slavery
William Thompson and Anna Wheeler
With a new introduction by the Rt Hon. Michael Foot and Marie Mulvey Roberts
ISBN 1 85506 247 X : 256pp : 1825 edition : £14.75

A Blighted Life: A True Story
Rosina Bulwer Lytton
With a new introduction by Marie Mulvey Roberts
ISBN 1 85506 248 8 : 178pp : 1880 edition : £10.75

The Beth Book
Sarah Grand
With a new introduction by Sally Mitchell
ISBN 1 85506 249 6 : 560pp : 1897 edition : £18.75

The Journal of a Feminist
Elsie Clews Parsons
With a new introduction and notes by Margaret C. Jones
ISBN 1 85506 250 X : 142pp : New edition : £12.75

Also available as a 5 volume set : ISBN 1 85506 261 5
Special set price : £65.00

MICHAEL FOOT
is the ex-leader of the Labour Party and for many years was the Member of Parliament for Blaenau Gwent. He is the author of numerous books including the life of Swift, *The Pen and the Sword* (1957), *Aneurin Bevan* (1962–73) and *The Politics of Paradise: A Vindication of Byron* (1988).

Marie Mulvey Roberts is a Senior Lecturer in literary studies at the University of the West of England and is the author of *British Poets and Secret Societies* (1986), and *Gothic Immortals* (1990). From 1994 she has been the co-editor of a Journal: 'Women's Writing; the Elizabethan to the Victorian Period', and the General Editor for three series: *Subversive Women, For Her Own Good*, and *Her Write His Name*. The volumes she has co-edited include: *Sources of British Feminism* (1993), *Perspectives on the History of British Feminism* (1994), *Controversies in the History of British Feminism* (1995) and *Literature and Medicine during the Eighteenth Century* (1993). Among her single edited books are, *Out of the Night: Writings from Death Row* (1994), and editions of Rosina Bulwer Lytton's *A Blighted Life* (1994) and *Shells from the Sands of Time* (1995).

COVER ILLUSTRATION
The Wollaston Family *by William Hogarth*
Cover designed by Dan Broughton